PHILIP ALLAN

LITERATURE GUIDE

FOR GCSE

GREAT EXPECTATIONS
CHARLES DICKENS

Peter Morrisson

Series editor: Jeanette Weatherall

PHILIP ALLAN
UPDATES

Philip Allan Updates, an imprint of Hodder Education, an Hachette UK company, Market Place, Deddington, Oxfordshire OX15 0SE

Orders

Bookpoint Ltd, 130 Milton Park, Abingdon, Oxfordshire OX14 4SB
tel: 01235 827827
fax: 01235 400401
e-mail: education@bookpoint.co.uk
Lines are open 9.00 a.m.–5.00 p.m., Monday to Saturday, with a 24-hour message answering service. You can also order through the Philip Allan Updates website: www.philipallan.co.uk

© Peter Morrisson 2011
ISBN 978-1-4441-2155-1
First printed 2011

Impression number 5 4 3 2 1
Year 2016 2015 2014 2013 2012 2011

Cover photo reproduced by permission of gemenacom/Fotolia

Printed in Spain

Hachette UK's policy is to use papers that are natural, renewable and recyclable products and made from wood grown in sustainable forests. The logging and manufacturing processes are expected to conform to the environmental regulations of the country of origin.

Contents

Getting the most from this book and website

You may find it useful to read sections of this guide when you need them, rather than reading it from start to finish. For example, you may find it helpful to read the *Context* section before you start reading the novel, or to read the *Plot and structure* section in conjunction with the novel — whether to back up your first reading of it at school or college or to help you revise. The sections relating to assessments will be especially useful in the weeks leading up to the exam.

The following features have been used throughout this guide.

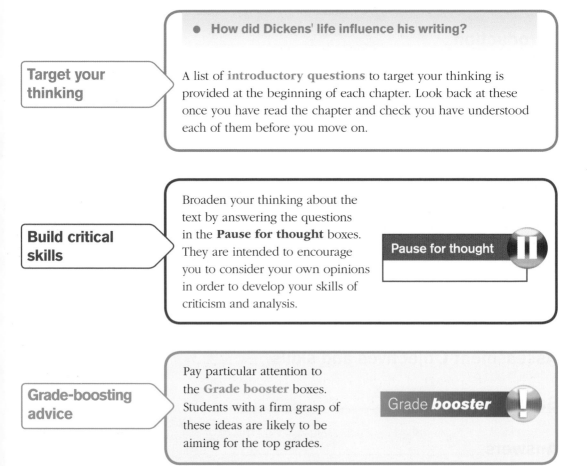

● **How did Dickens' life influence his writing?**

Target your thinking

A list of **introductory questions** to target your thinking is provided at the beginning of each chapter. Look back at these once you have read the chapter and check you have understood each of them before you move on.

Build critical skills

Broaden your thinking about the text by answering the questions in the **Pause for thought** boxes. They are intended to encourage you to consider your own opinions in order to develop your skills of criticism and analysis.

Pause for thought ❚❚

Grade-boosting advice

Pay particular attention to the **Grade booster** boxes. Students with a firm grasp of these ideas are likely to be aiming for the top grades.

Grade *booster* ❗

Key quotations are highlighted for you, and you may wish to use them as evidence in your examination answers. Page references are given for the Penguin Classics edition of the text (ISBN 978-0-14-143956-3). For each page reference, a chapter reference has also been given in case you are using a different edition.

> **Key quotation**
>
> 'I love her, I love her, I love her!'
>
> (Chapter 29, p. 243)

Be exam-ready

The **Grade focus** sections explain how you may be assessed and distinguish between higher and foundation responses.

Grade *focus* **!**

Get the top grades

Use the **Text focus** boxes to practise evaluating the text in detail and looking for evidence to support your understanding.

Text **focus**

Develop evaluation skills

Review your learning

Use the **Review your learning** sections to test your knowledge after you have read each chapter. Answers to the questions are provided in the final section of the guide.

Test your knowledge

Don't forget to go online for even more free revision activities and self-tests: **www.philipallan.co.uk/literatureguidesonline**

Introduction

How to approach the text

A novel is, above all, a narrative. A large part of the storyteller's art is to make you want to find out what happens next — to keep you reading to the end. In order to study *Great Expectations* and to enjoy it, you need to keep a close track of the events that take place in it. This guide will help you to do that, but you may also benefit from keeping your own notes on the main events and who is involved in them.

However, any novel consists of much more than its events. You need to know the story well in order to get a good grade in the exam, but if you spend a lot of time simply retelling the story you will not get a high mark. You also need to keep track of a number of other features.

First, you need to take notice of the settings in the novel (where the events take place) and how these influence the story. You also need to get to know the characters and be aware of how Dickens lets us know what they are like. Notice what they say and do, and what other people say about them. Think about why they behave in the way they do (their motives) and what clues the author gives us about this.

As you read on, you will notice themes: the ideas explored by the author in the book. You may find it easier to think about these while not actually reading the book, especially if you discuss them with other people. You should try to become aware of the style of the novel, especially on a second reading. This means how the author tells the story.

All these aspects of the novel are dealt with in this guide. However, you should always try to notice them for yourself. This guide is no substitute for a careful and thoughtful reading of the text.

Extra website information

For a detailed timeline of the events in *Great Expectations* plus additional analyses of characters and themes, please visit www.philipallan.co.uk/literatureguidesonline. Then go to the Downloads section for *Great Expectations*.

Context

The 'context' of a novel means the circumstances in which it was written — the social, historical and literary factors that influenced what the author wrote. All literature is influenced by the life experiences of the author and these are shaped by the world in which he/she lived. Therefore, in order to truly understand *Great Expectations* (1860–61), it is necessary to have some understanding of both Dickens' life and Dickens' world.

Charles Dickens' life

Early years

Charles Dickens was born in Portsmouth on 7 February 1812. His father, John Dickens, was a clerk in the Naval Pay Office and his mother, Elizabeth, had been a housekeeper to the wealthy Lord Crewe. In 1817, the family relocated to Chatham in Kent where they lived until 1822. The nearby city of Rochester later became the model for Pip's home town in *Great Expectations*, from which Pip takes the coach to and from London. In 1821, while living at Chatham, Dickens attended a local school run by a Baptist minister and proved to be a most able pupil.

Charles Dickens.

Lebrecht Music and Arts Photo Library/Alamy

In 1822, the family again relocated, this time to the great metropolis of London. The shock of this move to the young Charles may well be reflected in Pip's account of his first encounter with the city, in which he is overwhelmed by the 'immensity of London' (Chapter 20, p. 163). In 1824, John Dickens fell into debt and, apart from Charles, the entire family was incarcerated in the Marshalsea Debtors' Prison in London. This dark period of Charles Dickens' young life influenced a number of his later novels and clearly illustrates how a writer's art is influenced by personal experience.

The impact of debt

The theme of debt occurs in *David Copperfield* (1849–50). In this novel, Mr Micawber, modelled on John Dickens, is a kindly but financially incompetent man who painfully struggles to make his income cover his expenses. Similarly, *Little Dorrit* (1855–57) features a heroine, Amy Dorrit, whose father has spent many years imprisoned in the Marshalsea Debtors' Prison.

Great Expectations (1860–61) also explores the tragic potential of debt. On arriving in London, Pip describes being shown 'the Debtors' Door, out of which culprits came to be hanged' (Chapter 20, p. 166). Debt also becomes a major feature in Pip's own life. He only escapes imprisonment because of the generosity of Joe who selflessly clears all of his bills (Chapter 57).

After three months of being incarcerated in the Marshalsea, John Dickens managed to liberate himself and his family as a result of a fortunately timed inheritance.

The shoe blacking factory

During the period of the family's incarceration, a relative of Elizabeth Dickens tried to assist the family by arranging for young Charles to begin work in Warren's shoe blacking business. Just as he reached twelve, this sensitive and highly intelligent boy had to forgo his education in order to begin monotonous days spent packaging bottles of shoe polish for six shillings a week.

Although Dickens only had to endure this menial occupation for a matter of months, it left an indelible impression on his mind. As with debt, child exploitation became a major theme in his novels. *Oliver Twist* (1837–39) deals with the ruthless mistreatment of children throughout Victorian society, from corrupt workhouses, to heartless employers, to an insensitive and uncaring legal system. *David Copperfield* (1849–50), Dickens' most autobiographical novel, touches closely on his own personal experience at Warren's. Aged ten, David Copperfield is withdrawn from school by his cruel stepfather, Mr Murdstone, and sent to labour in a wine bottling factory. David works six days a week, from 7.00 a.m. until 8.00 p.m., for six shillings a week.

Great Expectations also pursues this theme. Like the young Charles Dickens, the youthful Pip hankers after an education and a higher social status than that afforded him as a blacksmith's apprentice. It is clear, however, that the mature Pip who narrates the novel admires Joe Gargery's thrift and industry.

Education and social advancement

Not long after his family's release from prison, Dickens was removed from his detested employment. In 1825 he resumed his schooling, attending Wellington House Academy in London as a day pupil. In 1827, at the age of 15, he began work as a clerk in an attorney's office. Only 18 months later, he set out as a freelance reporter in the court of Doctors' Commons.

Dickens' various experiences of the law also affected his writing. The corruption, insensitivity or incompetence of the legal profession became another major focus in his novels. Dickens' greatest indictment of the legal system occurs in *Bleak House* (1852–53), in which the self-serving legal profession slowly grinds down the financial resources and spiritual wellbeing of all those who pursue a disputed will. For an analysis of Dickens' treatment of the law in *Great Expectations*, see p. 43 of this guide.

Dickens was able to advance his own position in life to that of a freelance reporter because he had received an education as a child and because he had sufficient ambition to teach himself shorthand. By 1834, he had risen still further and joined the staff of the *Morning Chronicle*. In 1836, he began to publish, in serialised form, his first novel, *The Pickwick Papers*. Pickwick won him fame and success and firmly established his career as a novelist by the age of just 25. It is no wonder, therefore, that education is such an important theme in so many of Dickens' novels.

Falling in love

In 1857, Dickens met and fell in love with a young actress called Ellen Ternan. The following year, he separated from his wife of 22 years, Catherine, with whom he had had ten children. In 1860, he sold his London home and moved to Gad's Hill Place, which is a large mansion that he had purchased in 1856 and which is on the outskirts of Rochester and close to his boyhood home of Chatham.

Again, it is possible to see the close relationship between Dickens' life and his work. As mentioned earlier, Pip's home town is based on

Rochester. Furthermore, *Great Expectations* centres on Pip's deep and romantic attachment to Estella, thus enabling Dickens to express his own deep and romantic attachment to Ellen Ternan in fictional form. *Our Mutual Friend*, written during the years 1864–65, also has a deep and romantic attachment at its centre.

In 1870, before he was able to complete his last novel, *Edwin Drood*, Dickens died of a heart attack brought on by overwork. By the time of his death, voting rights had been greatly extended (1867), the practice of imprisonment for debt had been abolished (1869) and Forster's Elementary Education Act (1870) had set about creating the genesis of the state education system that we enjoy today. However, England still had a deeply unequal and class-ridden society, with tremendous excesses of both poverty and wealth, which would remain for many decades to come.

Dickens' world

During Charles Dickens' lifetime, nineteenth-century Britain was under tremendous pressure from the twin forces of science and technology, which generated great social, political and economic changes. These affected the ways in which the people of the time viewed themselves, their relationships with each other, their relationship with God and their relationship with society at large.

Pause for thought

Those of us fortunate enough to live in present-day Britain are reaping the benefits created by several centuries of industrialisation. However, in many less developed societies people are still suffering the same kinds of hardship and injustice that our ancestors were forced to endure when Charles Dickens was alive. Think about the relevance of the theme of industrialisation for modern readers of *Great Expectations*.

Industrialisation

Industrialisation was, in particular, a destabilising factor that threatened the entire fabric of Victorian England. It created great wealth for a new entrepreneurial minority who were astute enough to set up factories and mills or who created other related businesses that advanced Britain's trade and commerce. However, it also led to a ruthless exploitation of the largely unskilled and uneducated workers who were needed as manual labour to keep the machines running.

Social unrest

The new factory towns concentrated large numbers of workers into confined spaces. At the same time, workers inevitably became resentful of the poverty and suffering they were forced to endure by the wealthy manufacturers or mill owners who employed them. This had the effect of politicising people.

In 1838, the newly published *People's Charter* demanded, among other things, the right to vote for all men. The Chartist movement was divided as to the best means of achieving its aims — moral force or physical force? On 10 April 1848, a petition of some two million signatures in support of the *People's Charter* (although Chartists claimed to have six million signatures) was brought to London by around 150,000 Chartists. London was heavily fortified and the Royal Family fled to the Isle of Wight. In contrast with mainland Europe, where a series of revolutions was over-throwing the autocratic governments of the day, the Chartist protest ended peacefully.

In *Hard Times* (1854), Dickens explicitly explores the plight of people living in English factory towns, coping with the twin evils of poverty and pollution. In *A Tale of Two Cities* (1859), he evokes the horrors of the French Revolution of 1789 and explores the dangers of a society in which an unjust and heartless hierarchy is overthrown by an outraged and bloodthirsty rebellion. In both of these novels Dickens shows a clear appreciation of how poverty and oppression can drive people to desperate measures. There is an implicit appreciation of the fact that in order for British society to avoid the type of anarchy and self-destruction of the French Revolution, those in power need to be far more responsive to the basic human rights of the teeming masses below them.

Of course, Dickens was not the only novelist of his day exposing the evils of exploitation and oppression. Elizabeth Gaskell (1810–65) provided an even greater documentary vision of urban poverty and exploitation in her groundbreaking novel *Mary Barton* (1848). Later on in the century, Thomas Hardy (1840–1928) explored the brutal struggle for survival in the countryside in such novels as *Tess of the d'Urbervilles* (1891). As with Dickens, both lament the lack of decency within the ruling elite, whether they be ruthless factory owners or mean-spirited landed gentry.

The impact of science

Throughout the Victorian era, scientific discoveries began to undermine the traditional Christian beliefs and values which were commonly regarded as essential for social cohesion. The revolutionary thinker Karl Marx had explicitly acknowledged this when he wrote 'Religion…is the opium of the people' (1843–44). Marx meant that the promise of an afterlife encouraged the poor to suffer the iniquities and inequalities of this life in silence.

One of the biggest blows to traditional Christianity came with the publi-cation of Charles Darwin's *On the Origin of Species* (1859). Darwin argued for a model of the world in which life gradually evolved over an immense period of time. The idea of this incremental process challenged the

fundamental Christian belief that God created all things in just six days. Darwin's theory, being partly based on fossil evidence, also suggested that the world was many times older than the Bible indicated. If the Bible could not be trusted on this crucial point concerning the creation of life, what other errors might it contain?

A further impact of Darwin's findings was to suggest a world in which the predominant principle is 'the Survival of the Fittest'. This is a vision of an uncaring universe in which the weak are destroyed by the strong and in which God does not intervene. A number of these ideas had already surfaced prior to Darwin's publication. They had obviously influenced the famous poet Alfred Tennyson when he wrote of 'Nature, red in tooth and claw' in his epic poem *In Memoriam* (published in 1850).

The 1851 Census showed that church attendance was in decline. According to the historian H. C. G. Matthew, writing in the *Oxford Illustrated History of Britain*, 'Of potential church-goers, over five and a quarter million stayed at home.' This was out of a combined population of England and Wales of around 18 million. Matthew Arnold laments this trend towards greater secularisation in his famous poem 'Dover Beach' (1867) when he writes:

> The Sea of Faith
> Was once, too, at the full, and round earth's shore...
> But now I only hear
> Its melancholy, long withdrawing roar,
> Retreating...

Pause for thought

Dickens' heroes and heroines often display overtly Christian values. Think about the use of Christian imagery in the characterisation of Joe in *Great Expectations*. Then consider the relevance of this topic for Victorian readers of the novel.

Grade *booster*

A society or person can be described as secular when it does not place too much importance on religious beliefs and values. The process of secularisation, over time, can lead to a society where atheism or agnosticism is more usual than religion. To most Victorians, this prospect would have been horrific and Dickens' heroes and heroines typically display Christian values.

Population growth and urban development

Much pressure on Victorian society was also created by tremendous population growth during the nineteenth century. In 1801, according to the official census of that year, the population of England stood at 8.3 million. By the 1851 Census, it had more than doubled to 16.92 million. This growth was mainly in the towns and was supplemented by agricultural labourers leaving rural areas in search of higher wages or employment. For the first time in the history of the nation, more people in the UK mainland were living in towns and cities than in the countryside. Great Britain had become the leading manufacturing nation in the world. Again writing in

the *Oxford Illustrated History of Britain*, the historian H. C. G. Matthew remarks: 'An urban nation had no precedent: perhaps that was why the British dwelt so tenaciously on rural images and traditions.'

It can be argued that Dickens is dwelling on rural traditions in *Great Expectations* (1860–61). He deliberately sets his novel at the beginning of the century when 'Steam, was yet in its infancy' (Chapter 7, p. 46). In contrast with some of his other work, this novel does not focus in particular on the malignant physical institutions of Victorian society. Instead, and more importantly perhaps, it considers the condition of the nation's soul which has allowed such evils to evolve. *Great Expectations* presents a deeply poetic psychological study of a nation gripped by greed and selfishness. This is most powerfully explored through the concept of what it is to be a gentleman.

Is *Great Expectations* still relevant today?

Unlike the period when the novel was written, our society provides a welfare state with all the benefits of a state education system, a national health service, social security, old age pensions, universal suffrage and guaranteed human rights. Discrimination on the basis of social class is also, by and large, a thing of the past.

One similarity, however, is that our society appears to have replaced an obsession with the social elite of 'high society' for an obsession with the new aristocracy of celebrity. In addition, Pip's search for a meaningful, productive and morally upright life is as important today as it ever has been. The fundamental moral truths that Pip discovers on his way to full maturity help to establish this coming-of-age bildungsroman as the timeless classic that it has become.

Grade *booster*

A bildungsroman is a novel that explores the development of the personality of the main character. *Great Expectations* can correctly be described as a bildungsroman, and an examiner will be pleased to see such literary terminology in your work.

Grade *focus*

Knowing how the culture and society of the day influenced an author will raise your grade, but interrupting your literature examination with a mini history essay will not.

For a grade A, candidates should identify and comment on the impact of the social, cultural and historical contexts of texts on different readers at different times.

To gain an A*, you would need to fulfil all the grade-A requirements plus include what examiners describe as the additional quality of 'flair'. This means that little something extra that makes your answer stand out from the crowd.

For a grade C, candidates should show awareness of some of the social, cultural and historical contexts of texts and of how this influences their meanings for contemporary and modern readers.

The emphasis is on using the background historical information in order to analyse the novel's impact on the reader both now and when the novel was written. For example, the class divide between Pip and Estella may not be especially relevant to readers today, but the timeless theme of unrequited love certainly is.

Review your learning

(Answers are given on p. 91.)

1. During which years did Charles Dickens live?
2. In what way is Rochester significant to *Great Expectations*?
3. In what year did the young Charles Dickens and his family move to London?
4. Which two related childhood events are powerfully reflected in a number of his novels?
5. How might Dickens' personal circumstances have affected the romantic nature of *Great Expectations*?
6. In *Great Expectations*, how might Dickens be responding to his society's increasing lack of religious belief?

More interactive questions and answers online.

Plot and structure

- When is *Great Expectations* set?
- How does Dickens distort time within the novel?
- What are the main events in the novel and when do they occur?
- How does Dickens create and satisfy suspense?

Time frame

Main events

The main events of the novel take place over a period of approximately 16 years. Dickens' *working notes*, in which he initially planned out the timescale of the novel, state that 'Pip was about 7 at the opening of the story' (p. 510 of the Penguin Classics edition). This is confirmed within the novel itself when Pip tells Herbert in Chapter 50 that he thinks he was in his 'seventh year' when he first encountered Magwitch, although this phrase could equally identify Pip as having been six. At the beginning of Chapter 39, Pip announces that he is 23. This is the year of Magwitch's return, in which he reveals that he is Pip's true benefactor. Most of Volume III relates the events that unfold during the course of this turbulent year.

As Dickens is rather cavalier with his references to time, it is not always possible precisely to locate an event within the internal time frame of the novel. This is particularly so in Volume I. Pip is indentured to Joe approximately two years after the novel has begun. This would make him nine. However, according to Dickens' *working notes*, Pip is 'say 18 or 19' (p. 509) when he first arrives in London and, as his apprenticeship lasts just short of four years, the age at which he is apprenticed to Joe is more likely to be 14 or 15.

Historical setting

The exact year in which *Great Expectations* begins is also difficult to determine, as it is stated neither within the novel itself nor in Dickens' *working notes*. On the opening page of the novel, Dickens simply refers to a time 'long before the days of photographs' (p. 3). Other historical information that the mature Pip reveals during the course of his narrative enables the time of the main action to be fixed to the early nineteenth century.

One such recurrent historical theme is the mode of transport that Pip uses when he commutes between London and his home town. He travels to London for the first time at the beginning of Volume II. He states, 'The journey from our town to the metropolis, was a journey of about five hours' and the means of transport was a 'four-horse stage-coach' (Chapter 20, p. 163). Railways are never mentioned in the novel and as the first passenger railway opened in 1825, and Britain's rail network was virtually complete by 1850, the reader can clearly see that the young Pip's world is of an earlier period.

Using such historical details as mentioned above, the literary critic Jerome Meckier has concluded that the novel opens on Christmas Eve 1812, which is also the year of Dickens' birth. (See the editor's first note to Volume I, Chapter 1 on p. 485 of the Penguin Classics edition of *Great Expectations*.) Regardless of the exact date, it is clear that *Great Expectations* reflects the time of Dickens' own childhood when he was living in Chatham in Kent during 1817–22, which might be one reason why he has chosen to write the novel from the first-person perspective.

Structure

Great Expectations is divided into three volumes and each volume recounts a discreet phase in Pip's life. The novel was originally published in serial form between December 1860 and August 1861 in weekly instalments in Dickens' own weekly magazine entitled *All the Year Round*. The serial form involved the necessity for maintaining the reader's commitment, hence the continual creation and recreation of suspense. Furthermore, the fact that it was published in December will undoubtedly have influenced Dickens to open the novel on Christmas Eve so as to capitalise on the festive spirit.

Volume I

Chapters 1–6

The novel opens on Christmas Eve with the introduction of the main character, Pip, as a child. The narrative voice is immediately established as a first-person narrator looking back on an early childhood memory.
A sense of foreboding is created by the fact that Pip is visiting a graveyard, which contrasts with the festive nature of the season. The surroundings are made more threatening because 'this bleak place [was] overgrown with nettles...' (Chapter 1, p. 3). The fact that his parents are dead instantly

Pause for thought

Think about the ways in which high-profile television shows such as *Lost* and *24* create, satisfy and then recreate new strands of suspense as they build towards an end of series climax. Now chart the progress of one line of suspense in *Great Expectations*. Do the points of climax always appear at the end of a chapter or volume?

establishes Pip as an orphan and so creates sympathy for him. Tension and suspense are introduced when Pip is surprised by a convict who manhandles him roughly and threatens to cut his throat. Pip's obvious terror heightens the dramatic impact of the situation.

Pip meets Magwitch in the graveyard.

ITV/Rex Features

Grade *booster*

The immediate creation of suspense in Chapter 1 is essential, especially as the novel appeared in episodes rather like a modern-day soap opera or long-running drama series. Dickens needed to generate questions in his readers' minds so that they would follow the next episode in order to discover the answers.

The convict, whom we later discover is named Magwitch, terrorises the seven-year-old Pip into agreeing to steal food and a file from his foster parents, Joe and Mrs Joe Gargery. This causes a crisis of conscience in the boy, and creates an internal psychological dynamic which drives the plot throughout most of these early chapters. Pip is torn between his promise to Magwitch and the love and respect he feels for Joe. He is also terrified of being beaten by Mrs Joe should she discover the theft. Mrs Joe's violence is well established in this section and so the reader knows that Pip's fears are well founded. However, Dickens' treatment of this violence is comical and so is it not as disturbing to the reader as it might have been.

The suspense aroused by Pip's dilemma is finally resolved in Chapter 5 when Magwitch deliberately takes the blame for the thefts, although Pip's sense of guilt over stealing from Joe persists. However, the suspense created by the obvious hatred between the two convicts, Magwitch and

Key quotation

The terrors that had assailed me whenever Mrs. Joe had gone near the pantry, or out of the room, were only to be equalled by the remorse with which my mind dwelt on what my hands had done.

(Chapter 4, p. 23)

Compeyson, is not resolved. This leaves a question in the reader's mind that is not answered until Volume III.

Although the reader is not aware of it yet, Dickens has introduced a plot element which becomes highly significant at the end of Volume I. Pip's 'noble' behaviour has a serious effect on Magwitch, who determines to reciprocate by making Pip a gentleman.

The powerful motif of the 'mist', which symbolises moral blindness, is also introduced in this section. The 'hulks' reinforce this impression and stand as a powerful symbol of crime and punishment.

Grade booster

A motif is a recurring image or idea. Try to introduce literary terminology like this into your work.

> **Key quotation**
>
> The mist was heavier yet when I got out upon the marshes, so that instead of my running at everything, everything seemed to run at me.
>
> (Chapter 3, p. 17)

Pause for thought

Why is mist such a good symbol for expressing losing sight of the right thing to do? What other symbols could have been used?

The bridal dining room at Satis House.

Chapters 7–13

A year has passed. Dickens now introduces a new situation that generates a new area of suspense for the reader and drives the action in this section of the novel. Pip learns that he is to visit a local rich lady, Miss Havisham.

Pip arrives at Satis House, a decaying mansion that has a strong gothic atmosphere to it. He is met by the rude and arrogant Estella who instantly sets about insulting him. So begins the process of undermining his self-esteem which ultimately results in his obsession with bettering himself so that he can be worthy of her. Although distressed by her behaviour, Pip is captivated by Estella's beauty and falls instantly in love. This is the start of the romantic interest. The reader's desire to

> **Key quotation**
>
> She seemed much older than I, of course, being a girl, and beautiful and self-possessed; and she was as scornful of me as if she had been one-and-twenty, and a queen.
>
> (Chapter 8, p. 56)

ITV/Rex Features

know if Pip will eventually 'win' Estella is one of the most compelling areas of suspense in the novel.

Miss Havisham is immediately established as a fascinating figure who creates significant suspense by her bizarre appearance and behaviour. Dickens sets about gradually establishing the powerful misconception that she might be intending to advance Pip's prospects in life. This becomes a tremendous source of suspense later on in the novel when Pip does come into his 'great expectations'. Both Pip and the reader are led to believe that his benefactor is Miss Havisham and, therefore, that he must be destined to be with Estella.

> **Key quotation**
>
> **Then, he and my sister would pair off in such nonsensical speculations about Miss Havisham, and about what she would do with me and for me...**
>
> (Chapter 12, p. 97)

Grade *booster*

'Gothic' refers to a type of novel that was popular in the nineteenth century. It was a style that encompassed such elements as spooky old houses, mad people and mysterious events. Dickens is using aspects of the genre in his portrayal of Miss Havisham.

> **Pause for thought** ⏸
>
> Miss Havisham is an excellent example of Dickens' ability to create suspense not just by plot but also by characterisation. The reader is intrigued to discover the reasons behind her strange behaviour. Why have all the clocks been stopped at 'twenty minutes to nine'? Why is she wearing a faded wedding dress?

Chapter 11 introduces the reader to Herbert Pocket, the 'pale young gentleman' who challenges Pip to fight. Herbert remains an undeveloped character at this stage.

Important themes are first developed in this section, such as revenge and class. As a result of her obsessive desire to avenge herself on all males, Miss Havisham tacitly encourages Estella to make Pip feel ashamed of his working-class roots and so begins his drive to become a gentleman. However, the run-down condition of both Miss Havisham's appearance and her house send out powerful clues to the reader that Pip's ambition is not worthwhile.

Grade *booster* ❗

Dickens is able to mislead the reader regarding Miss Havisham's intentions for Pip and Estella because of his skilful use of a first-person narrator. Novelists often use unreliable first-person narrators.

Chapters 14–19

Dickens moves time on again in this section. At the beginning of Chapter 14, approximately one year has passed since Pip's first visit to Satis House. Pip has begun to train as Joe's apprentice but the position that he had long looked forward to is now hateful to him owing to his desire to be worthy of Estella. However, Estella will not reappear again until Volume II as she has been sent abroad to be educated as a lady. There is a deliberate parallel here in their respective careers that emphasises their different social status.

The important themes of longing to be a gentleman and of self-improvement through education are significantly enhanced in this section. Dickens' writing is more psychologically based than action based as the main dynamic is in Pip's mind: his struggle to come to terms with his humble life as a blacksmith's apprentice.

However, Dickens returns to a more robust and action-based plot line at the end of Chapter 15 when Mrs Joe has been savagely attacked. In Chapter 16 Biddy declares the culprit to be Orlick but nothing conclusive is given away, again creating an area of suspense that helps to keep the reader engaged.

The plot gathers tremendous pace towards the end of Volume I when Pip is in the fourth year of his apprenticeship. Jaggers suddenly appears in Chapter 18 and announces that Pip has come into 'great expectations' and is to leave for London in a week to become a gentleman. Jaggers' non-committal suggestion of Matthew Pocket, Miss Havisham's relative, as Pip's tutor reopens the romantic suspense of whether Pip will finally obtain Estella. It also reinforces the deliberate deception which encourages the reader to believe that Miss Havisham is Pip's benefactor.

Pip's attitude and behaviour abruptly become distant to Joe and Biddy as he prepares to move into a much higher level of society, one which would ridicule him for having such humble acquaintances. This is not only the beginning of a new phase in Pip's life but it is also the expansion of one of the novel's major themes and social comments. Through Pip's deplorable attitude towards those who have cared for him, Dickens begins to show the reader the shallow, unproductive and snobbish lifestyle that being a gentleman involves. It is not until Volume III that Pip will come to a full realisation of this for himself and will understand how shameful his ingratitude has been.

Volume II

Chapters 20–26

In Chapter 20, Pip arrives in London and, according to Dickens' *working notes*, he is 'say 18 or 19' (p. 509). Dickens immediately qualifies Pip's excitement at arriving in London by depicting the city as both squalid and frightening. Just as 'mist' is a recurring motif in the marshes of Volume I, 'dirt' is a recurring motif in London. As with the opening to Volume I, death is immediately apparent.

One of Pip's first encounters in London is with the corrupt 'partially drunk minister of justice', who offers to reveal the full brutality of Newgate Prison for a price (Chapter 20, pp. 165–66).

> **Key quotation**
>
> **So, I came into Smithfield; and the shameful place, being all asmear with filth and fat and blood and foam, seemed to stick to me.**
>
> (Chapter 20, p. 165)

Newgate Prison.

TopFoto

> **Key quotation**
>
> **As I declined the proposal on the plea of an appointment, he was so good as to take me into a yard and show me where the gallows was kept, and also where people were publicly whipped...**
>
> (Chapter 20, p. 166)

Just as there was the dramatic foreshadowing of a gallows looming over Magwitch in Chapter 3 (p. 18), so there is a gallows here. By showing the savagery of the judicial system, Dickens is also introducing a theme that becomes extremely important towards the end of Volume III.

The fact that Pip has moved away from the limited confines of his home town also allows Dickens to introduce a host of new characters and so generate new areas of interest for the reader. For example, Jaggers' emphatic declaration that he is not permitted to reveal the identity of Pip's benefactor only serves to heighten this mystery — and it is not ultimately resolved until the end of this volume.

Chapters 21 and 22 reunite Pip with Herbert Pocket, the two having briefly met at Satis House when Herbert had challenged Pip to fight. The reader may be surprised to discover that Herbert is not the pugilistic boy of Pip's previous encounter but a caring and thoughtful young man. The occasion of their reunion allows Dickens the opportunity to satisfy some of the suspense that has been built up in Volume I. For example, we learn how Miss Havisham was jilted on her wedding day by a heartless opportunist and how she adopted and reared Estella 'to wreak revenge on all the male sex' (Chapter 22, p. 177).

Grade *booster*

Dramatic foreshadowing is when a writer provides subtle clues, often through imagery, which foretell future events. In Magwitch's case, the gallows are highly significant. This is an example of how carefully Dickens planned his novels.

As *Great Expectations* is a first-person narrative, the reader can only know what the narrator knows and so Dickens has to plan for occasional scenes like this in order to relay essential plot information. However, in the process of answering some questions, new ones are created. What has happened to the man who callously broke Miss Havisham's heart?

Dickens uses this series of chapters in order to introduce such additional characters as Matthew Pocket (Pip's tutor), Startop and Drummle. Drummle is quickly established as an aggressive and mean-spirited individual. He becomes an important plot device in Volume III when Dickens uses him to drive a seemingly immovable wedge between Pip and Estella. In dramatic terms, this can be termed a 'complication'. A new strand of suspense is also created in Chapter 26 with the introduction of Molly, Jaggers' enigmatic maid.

This series of chapters is much less dramatic than other sections of the novel and relies quite heavily on comedy for its momentum. Good examples are the hopelessly disorganised Pocket household and the eccentric home of Wemmick with its incongruous castle-like features and the amiable but deaf 'aged parent'.

Chapters 27–34

Dickens again moves the plot on by reintroducing Estella and Miss Havisham into Pip's life. There is much anticipation as to how Estella will react to Pip now that he is a gentleman and now that she has grown up into a young woman.

However, before developing this area of suspense, Dickens brings Joe to London to deliver the news of Estella's return from abroad (Chapter 27). This allows Dickens the opportunity to write another memorably comic scene as Joe awkwardly juggles his hat before Pip and Herbert. More importantly, it allows Dickens to highlight Pip's snobbishness and the depth of his ingratitude to Joe. Joe now feels so awkward in Pip's company that he begins the scene by referring to 'Pip' but soon feels compelled to address him as 'Sir' owing to the cold formality of his reception.

Key quotation

Estella: 'You must know...that I have no heart...'
(Chapter 29, p. 237)

Miss Havisham: 'Love her, love her, love her!'
(Chapter 29, p. 239)

Pip: 'I love her, I love her, I love her!'
(Chapter 29, p. 243)

The next day Pip hurriedly takes the coach to Satis House but, significantly, rejects Joe again by choosing to stay at the Blue Boar inn. There is a powerful reunion at Satis House in Chapter 29 in which Miss Havisham exhorts Pip to love Estella. Estella, in turn, warns Pip that she is incapable of love. Once again, the romantic interest in the novel becomes suspenseful. Pip clearly hopes that he and Estella are destined to be together, but Estella's declared inability to love creates a tremendous complication that the reader is most eager to have resolved.

Dickens also uses this trip to Satis House to have Pip arrange for Jaggers to sack Orlick from his post as Miss Havisham's gatekeeper. This seemingly minor event reaches a climax towards the end of Volume III, when Orlick tries to murder Pip. However, any sense of the future dramatic import of this event is masked by two comic scenes: Trabb's boy ridiculing Pip's social pretentiousness (Chapter 30), and Pip's visit to the theatre in London (Chapter 31) to see Wopsle star in *Hamlet*.

As is often the case with Dickens, the parody of Pip by Trabb's boy has a satirical purpose. As Trabb's boy chants 'Don't know yah!' (Chapter 30, p. 246) the reader is reminded of Pip's rejection of Joe and Biddy.

After the comic interlude, which allows Dickens to keep the reader in a state of anticipation, the main plot line involving Estella and Pip is resumed in Chapter 33. Dickens deliberately creates suspense when he has Estella remark: 'We are not free to follow our own devices, you and I' (p. 265). By this, Dickens is subtly confirming to the reader Pip's hopeful impression that he and Estella are destined by Miss Havisham to marry. However, Dickens then almost immediately throws the reader into confusion by re-establishing tension when Estella remarks 'will you never take warning?' (p. 268).

In Chapter 34, Pip is 'generalising a period of my life' (p. 274) and, by Chapter 36, two or more years have passed on and Pip is 21. Dickens resumes his social commentary when he has the narrator reveal the ridiculously extravagant and unproductive lifestyle of a gentleman as Pip and Herbert spiral into debt.

Chapters 35–39

Chapter 35 contains the riotously funny description of Mrs Joe's funeral, which includes such comic moments as the bystanders cheering the procession because they are so thrilled by the over-the-top spectacle of the occasion. However, Dickens also uses the event to remind the reader of Pip's continuing neglect of Joe.

Chapter 36, when Pip reaches his twenty-first birthday, continues the important theme of Pip's ever-increasing debts. However, the reader is also reminded of Pip's fundamental good nature as in Chapter 37 he uses his wealth to help Herbert gain an advantageous position in Clarriker's merchant business.

Grade *booster*

A parody is a comical imitation. Trabb's boy is a parody of Pip because he is imitating Pip's assumed social superiority in order to suggest how ridiculous Pip has become.

Key quotation

Estella: 'And necessarily,' she added, in a haughty tone; 'what was fit company for you once, would be quite unfit company for you now.'
(Chapter 29, p. 237)

Grade *booster*

Satire is when a writer uses humour to make a moral point by making fun of the vice or folly of someone or something. Pip's folly is to reject those who love him because they are not suitable company for a gentleman.

Key quotation

At length, the thing being done, and he having that day entered Clarriker's House, and he having talked to me for a whole evening in a flush of pleasure and success, I did really cry in good earnest when I went to bed, to think that my expectations had done some good to somebody.
(Chapter 37, p. 299)

In Chapter 38, Dickens discreetly moves time on two years. The tension of the novel's main romantic interest is maintained, as Pip's jealousy intensifies over Estella's increasing circle of male admirers, especially the detestable Drummle. Another source of dramatic interest in this section is the first sign of a rift between Estella and Miss Havisham. This occurs in Chapter 38 when Miss Havisham ironically scolds Estella for her lack of affection.

By Chapter 39, Pip is 23. This chapter does exactly what Chapter 19 did: it ends the volume on a climax related to Pip's great expectations, except this time it dashes rather than exacerbates Pip's hopes. Magwitch's unexpected return on a symbolically stormy night reveals that he, rather than Miss Havisham, is Pip's benefactor. Once again Dickens satisfies an area of suspense for the reader at the end of the volume. But, again, the resolution is really a complication which raises a new question mark over Pip's future with Estella and this propels the reader into Volume III.

Volume III

Chapters 40–57 deal in great detail with the period from January to June of the year in which Pip has become 23.

Chapters 58–59 cover a period of 11 years and briefly summarise the time leading up to the climactic moment when Pip and Estella unexpectedly meet at the site of the former Satis House and finally become united. Both characters are approximately 34.

Chapters 40–44

Despite Magwitch's rough manners, the obvious delight he shows in Pip in Chapter 39 instantly establishes him as a sympathetic figure. Both suspense and concern are generated in Chapter 40 by Pip's discovery of a mysterious figure lurking in the darkness of the staircase only hours after Magwitch's arrival. This creates tension as the reader is aware that Magwitch is an illegal returnee and faces the death penalty should he be caught.

Text focus

Read the extract on p. 332 of Chapter 40 which begins 'There's something worth spending in that there book…' and ends 'Look over it, dear boy'. Consider the various ways in which Dickens shows Magwitch's self-reproaching humility and obvious affection for Pip and further consider how this endears Magwitch to the reader.

Once more, Pip is displayed in a poor light as yet again his ingratitude and snobbery come to the fore. It is important that Dickens establishes Pip's negative reaction to Magwitch at the outset of Volume III. Much of the dramatic interest, as well as the moral message, arising out of the rest of the novel results from the change of attitude that Pip will undergo during the next three months of his life.

Chapter 42 is yet another example of an episode that Dickens deliberately has to create in order to update Pip, and hence the reader, on crucial plot information which has so far been withheld. Magwitch recounts his history with Compeyson, the man we saw him grappling with on the marshes in Chapter 5. We also learn that it was Compeyson who jilted Miss Havisham on her wedding day. This carefully planned revelation allows Dickens to satisfy two significant areas of suspense at one time. However, the current whereabouts of Compeyson still remain a mystery and, therefore, add further tension as to the identity of the suspicious lurker mentioned in Chapter 40.

Pip's resolution to visit Satis House to say goodbye to Estella creates tremendous anticipation. The reader eagerly looks forward to seeing Pip challenge Miss Havisham over her cruel deception. The confrontation is genuinely electrifying and Miss Havisham displays uncharacteristic signs of guilt. The great power of the scene is further enhanced by Estella's revelation that she is to marry Drummle.

Text focus

Read the following extract from Chapter 44, p. 360: 'But when I fell into the mistake I have so long remained in…' to 'Waiting until she was quiet again — for this, too, flashed out of her in a wild and sudden way — I went on.' Look carefully at Dickens' use of highly charged emotive vocabulary: for example, 'kind', 'snares', 'flashed', 'wild'. Also look at his use of short sentences, longer but heavily punctuated sentences, rhetorical questions and exclamation marks in the dialogue in order to convey both Pip's and Miss Havisham's agitation.

Grade *booster*

A rhetorical question is asked to create a desired effect rather than to gain an answer. The expected/preferred answer is assumed. Writers often use rhetorical questions to create a sense of engagement with the reader.

On his return to London at the end of Chapter 44, the suspense regarding Magwitch's safety is immediately reignited as Pip receives a climactic note from Wemmick warning: 'DON'T GO HOME'.

Chapters 45–49

The focus returns to Magwitch. The reader is reminded of the grave danger that Magwitch is in as Pip and Herbert take enhanced precautions for his safety by removing him to Clara's house. The comic interlude in

Chapter 47, Wopsle's latest dramatic performance, is also economically turned back onto the main action as Wopsle informs Pip that during the performance he had recognised a convict (Compeyson) sitting just behind Pip. In Chapter 48, Dickens satisfies a further area of suspense through Pip's certain conviction that Molly is Estella's real mother.

Chapter 49 returns us to Satis House for another dramatic scene with Miss Havisham. Her remorse for the harm that she has caused to both Pip and Estella is emotionally satisfying for the reader, and the fire creates both a literal and metaphorical climax. It is as if the intense hatred and desire for vengeance that she has harboured throughout the novel has finally consumed her.

An older Pip on a visit to Miss Havisham.

One of the most interesting features of the chapters in this section of the novel is that Pip has become far less egocentric and is now displaying a much deeper concern for others, including Miss Havisham and Magwitch. Pip's compassion for Miss Havisham is particularly admirable considering the way that she has treated him over the course of the novel.

Key quotation

In the moment when I was withdrawing my head to go quietly away, I saw a great flaming light spring up. In the same moment, I saw her running at me, shrieking, with a whirl of fire blazing all about her, and soaring at least as many feet above her head as she was high.

(Chapter 49, pp. 401–02)

Chapters 50–53

In Chapter 50, Dickens has Herbert relate to Pip more of Magwitch's past. This scene stretches the credibility of the first-person narrator. It involves Pip the narrator many years later recalling in tremendous detail what Herbert is similarly recalling in tremendous detail after his conversation with Magwitch the previous evening. But it is important that both Pip and the reader are given this information at this point because it allows Pip to make the startling deduction that Estella is Magwitch's daughter. Pip has uncovered a secret that had eluded even the astute and resourceful Jaggers.

For the first time, Pip is finally in full possession of the facts regarding Estella and this simultaneously suggests that he has become master of

PHILIP ALLAN LITERATURE GUIDE **FOR GCSE**

his own destiny, having at long last moved beyond the web of lies and deception which had ensnared him for so long. Pip's caring character is again emphasised in Chapters 51 and 52 when he finalises the financial arrangements that will secure Herbert's future even though his own financial outlook is bleak.

Having answered most of the outstanding questions raised in the plot, Dickens immediately creates a new source of suspense in the form of the mysterious letter which suggests that if Pip wishes to protect Magwitch then he must return to his home village. Pip responds to the summons forthwith and arrives at the meeting place, the sluice house, after dark later that night. Of course, it is a trap to enable Orlick to wreak a brutal revenge. It is also an opportunity for Dickens to tie up a few other loose ends, such as the identity of Mrs Joe's attacker.

As Orlick prepares to pummel Pip to death, it would appear that there is no escape. However, Dickens has already laid the ground for his protagonist to be saved. He had Pip casually mention at the end of Chapter 52 that he had lost the letter: 'I had previously sought in my pockets for the letter, that I might refer to it again, but I could not find it...' (p. 421). This little plot device allows Dickens to stage a credible last-minute rescue by Herbert, Startop and, ironically, Trabb's boy in Chapter 53.

Chapters 54–59

Pip's stoicism and his continued concern for Magwitch dominate Chapter 54. Despite his severe burns, Pip perseveres with the intention to board a steamer with Magwitch and leave the country. His good friends Herbert and Startop continue to assist him. Chapter 54 contains a beautiful and sustained description of the River Thames as they row towards what they hope will be safety. Nevertheless Dickens maintains the tension as Pip the narrator continually reports to the reader the group's fear of being followed.

In order to maximise dramatic intensity, Magwitch is indeed apprehended at the last moment — just as they can see the smoke from the Hamburg steamer. In the violent struggle that follows, Magwitch enacts his revenge upon Compeyson as the latter drowns. This scene closely parallels their fight scene in Chapter 5 but this time Dickens allows the reader the satisfaction of seeing Compeyson receive the fate that he so richly deserves. This scene concludes another strand of the novel with an action-packed climax.

> **Grade booster**
>
> A protagonist is the principle character.

> **Grade booster**
>
> 'Irony' has many meanings. Here it means 'the opposite of what might have been expected'. Trabb's boy's involvement is both ironic and amusing because, as Pip himself acknowledges, his dislike of Pip is such that saving Pip is not what he would have chosen to do had he realised exactly what was happening.

> **Grade booster**
>
> Stoicism means having the courage and strength of character to endure great suffering. Stoicism is especially admirable when that suffering is on behalf of another person.

Pip's attachment to Magwitch is patently clear in Chapters 55 and 56 as he supports Magwitch through his trial and nurses him until his death some ten days later. Chapter 57 reintroduces Joe who, in a parallel scene, nurses Pip and protects him from arrest. By uniting both Pip and Joe at this point in the novel, and by highlighting the similarity between them, Dickens shows how far Pip has developed as a moral being since the beginning of Volume III. This is further emphasised by the religious terms that Pip uses to describe Joe.

The full reconciliation with both Joe and Biddy occurs in Chapter 58 when Pip arrives shortly after their wedding, although there is the slight complication that he had intended to ask Biddy to marry him. The fact that Biddy marries Joe on the day that Pip was going to propose to her is yet another irony. Symbolically, the sun is shining: 'The June weather was delicious' (Chapter 58, p. 477). Pip has finally left behind the long winter of disharmony and discontent of his former life and is now able to blossom into the full moral being that Dickens had always intended him to be.

Chapter 59 briefly recounts the next 11 years of Pip's life in which he goes abroad to work with Herbert and becomes a productive and successful businessman as opposed to the unproductive and debt-ridden gentleman he had once been. The moment of his return to the forge 11 years on is laden with symbolism. It is December, the same month in which Pip's story began some 27 years previously. In one way, the novel has turned full circle as it returns both Pip and the reader to the place and month where it all began. Joe, of course, is sitting by the hearth but this time there is a different Pip and this one is surrounded by the love of Joe and Biddy; there is no Mrs Joe to spoil the picture.

The plot ends on a major coincidence. Pip revisits the site of the former Satis House and there meets Estella who also has not returned for 11 years. Estella is much wiser and chastened as she too has undergone a long and painful spiritual journey. Their romance is finally resolved at the scene of their first meeting. They are instantly reconciled and the last lines complete the love story which has been the driving force of most of the novel: '...I saw the shadow of no parting from her.'

Grade *focus*

When writing about *Great Expectations* in the exam, do not write long narrative accounts of what happens in the novel. A*–C grades require you to explain how aspects of language, structure and form affect readers — not to re-tell the story at length.

Review your learning

(Answers on p. 91)

1 In what year might the beginning of the novel be set?
2 What age is Pip at the beginning of the novel?
3 Approximately what age is he when he begins his apprenticeship?
4 What does 'suspense' mean?
5 Why does Dickens resolve a number of areas of suspense at fairly early stages in the novel?
6 How do the frequent comic interludes help to create suspense?

More interactive questions and answers online.

Characterisation

- **What is the difference between a 'rounded' character and a 'flat' character?**
- **Why does Charles Dickens create both types of character?**
- **What methods does he use to reveal his characters to the reader?**
- **What are the main characters like?**
- **For what purposes does Dickens use his characters?**

Characters and caricatures

In *Great Expectations*, as in all of Charles Dickens' novels, the reader is introduced to a wide array of characters that vary in the degree to which they can be acknowledged as 'real people' of the type that we encounter in everyday life. Dickens' 'rounded' characters are the fuller, three-dimensional figures, such as Pip and Estella. They resemble real people in that they are composed of many different personality traits which often conflict. Importantly, rounded characters are capable of change and growth. These tend to be the characters with whom we, as readers, are most emotionally involved.

However, there is another, far more populous, species of character in *Great Expectations*: the caricatures. A few of these are more developed and rounded than others, a good example being Joe. Generally, however, the caricatures are creatures who do not show much, if any, insight into the true nature of others or themselves. Therefore, their comments on the purpose of life, or the merits and demerits of other characters within the novel, can rarely be trusted. They are 'stock' characters who are rarely capable of change. They exhibit a restricted range of human thought, emotion and behaviour and are essentially used to illustrate a limited number of human characteristics such as greed, envy and self-interest. They are frequently employed in order to highlight a moral point or theme that the author wishes to express to the reader and they are often satirised and ridiculed for their own moral short-sightedness.

Such caricatures include Mrs Joe and Pumblechook. As well as providing moral instruction, both of these characters also help to create humour.

There are also the 'darker' caricatures such as Compeyson and Orlick. Both of these characters demonstrate that sin results in either death or imprisonment and their impact on the reader is designed to be much

PHILIP ALLAN LITERATURE GUIDE **FOR GCSE**

more serious. They help to create suspense because of the threat that they pose to the more sympathetic personalities within the novel. Furthermore, they fill the reader with a sense of moral outrage because of their cruel mistreatment of others.

How Dickens reveals character

The personality of a character can be revealed in a variety of ways:

- Actions — what the character does and how this affects other characters for good or ill.
- Dialogue — what the character says and what other characters say about that character.
- Thoughts — the secret unexpressed hopes, desires and perceptions that the character may inwardly conceive but does not wish to divulge to other characters. Of course, these are more difficult to reveal in a first-person narrative like *Great Expectations* as the narrator can only really have a detailed knowledge of his or her own thoughts and feelings. The reader is unlikely to tolerate too high a level of intuitive guesswork regarding the thoughts and feelings of other characters. Such a god-like omniscience (all knowledge) is more the preserve of a third-person narrator.
- The narrator — the observations of the narrator on the personality and behaviour of other characters.
- The author's use of imagery (metaphors, similes and personifications).

Great Expectations is a first-person narrative and, therefore, the reader should be wary of taking all of Pip's comments at face value. However, Dickens is clearly presenting the Pip who relates the story as an individual who has arrived at a deep spiritual and moral awareness and who is, therefore, somebody the reader can trust.

The character studies that follow use evidence derived from all of the above ways in which Dickens reveals his major characters to the reader.

Pip

- makes tremendous moral and spiritual growth throughout the novel
- has a natural nobility of speech and manner despite humble origins
- has a strong sense of right and wrong and is very much affected by conscience
- falls deeply in love with Estella from first sight
- desperately wishes to become a gentleman so as to be worthy of Estella's higher social status

Grade *booster*

Dickens often associates his characters with images that provide a strong clue as to their respective personalities.

Grade *booster*

Higher-tier exam questions often ask you to comment on how the author reveals aspects of a character's personality.

- suffers much unhappiness and dissatisfaction as a result of his infatuation with Estella
- becomes corrupted by the shallow values of status and wealth as he aspires to rise in society
- ultimately becomes ashamed of his own ungrateful and ungenerous behaviour towards Joe and Biddy
- rediscovers the natural affections of his original childhood self

Pip's name may well be symbolic of the emotional, intellectual and spiritual growth that he makes throughout the novel, a pip being a seed. This ability to evolve and grow distinguishes him from most of the other characters, who largely remain static.

In the opening sentence, Pip immediately introduces himself as the novel's narrator and sets about recounting the chance encounter with Magwitch that ultimately determines his fate. The older narrator describes his younger self as 'the small bundle of shivers' (Chapter 1, p. 4) who studies the graves of both of his parents and all five of his brothers. A number of sympathetic circumstances are immediately established: he is an orphan, he is frightened by the stormy weather, and he is about to be roughly manhandled by an apparently fierce and murderous convict.

In his dealings with Magwitch, the convict, Pip's essentially virtuous nature is instantly established. In response to Magwitch's rough questioning, the young Pip truthfully and respectfully recounts his family circumstances while simultaneously revealing a degree of spirit and courage which gains the reader's respect:

> I was dreadfully frightened, and so giddy that I clung to him with both hands, and said, 'If you would kindly please to let me keep upright, sir, perhaps I shouldn't be sick, and perhaps I could attend more.'
>
> (Chapter 1, p. 5)

The young Pip's words reveal impeccable good manners, a mature vocabulary and a sophisticated use of grammar that is generally lacking in Dickens' lower-class characters. This contrasts sharply with the clumsy sentence structures and often inaccurately pronounced vocabulary that Magwitch uses to terrorise Pip.

Through his absolute terror of Magwitch, Pip is forced to enter into a pact which involves the theft of food and a file from his foster parents, Joe and Mrs Joe Gargery. This promise causes an internal moral conflict which results in such an extreme degree of distress that it drives the plot for the first five chapters. Because the young Pip has such a highly developed sense of right and wrong, he is torn between keeping his promise to Magwitch and stealing from his beloved Joe. Dickens depicts this moral dilemma with an intensity far beyond what would be expected of a child of just seven years of age. Pip the narrator describes how his younger self agonises over 'the dreadful pledge I was under to commit a larceny on those sheltering premises...' (Chapter 2, p. 10).

The next significant event in Pip's moral and spiritual evolution is his first encounter with Estella at Satis House. This meeting proves to be the cause of young Pip's dissatisfaction with his life. Almost immediately, he begins to lose sight of his own moral compass and of the moral superiority of the person who had hitherto been most important to him, his loving but child-like foster father Joe.

His first encounter with Estella and Miss Havisham deludes him into mistaking arrogance and cruelty for superiority. This, combined with the young Estella's great beauty, results in an infatuation with prevails throughout the rest of the novel and which, until the latter stages, becomes the guiding principle which motivates Pip to seek social status over truth and integrity. Consequently, his proposed future as an apprentice at the forge, which had long been the dream of both Pip and Joe, now becomes viewed as demeaning.

As Pip's sense of shame at the sturdiness of Joe's working boots and the roughness of Joe's skilled blacksmith's hands suggests, only the shallow and unproductive life of a gentleman will suffice. Of course, Pip the narrator recognises the lack of wisdom in his younger self's hotly declared adolescent ambition when he immediately qualifies it as being a 'lunatic confession...' (Chapter 17, p. 129).

Towards the end of Volume I, Pip's wish to be a gentleman is indeed granted, this being part of the fairy-tale quality of the novel. However, as in most fairy tales, it is wise to be careful what you wish for. The life of a gentleman, as depicted in Volume II, leads Pip into profligate ways which quickly result in debt, depression and a lack of direction. Worse still, Pip's extravagant lifestyle also leads to the corruption of his best friend, the otherwise virtuous Herbert Pocket. Through Pip's severe lapses in both judgement and behaviour, Dickens demonstrates the moral inadequacies of the upper-class society into which Pip has successfully moved.

Ultimately, what restores Pip to the upright moral certainties that he possessed as a child is the knowledge that his status as a gentleman is

> ### Grade *booster*
>
> When writing about character in the exam, you are more likely to gain a higher grade if you use terms that show a precise understanding of specific aspects of personality: for example, words such as 'innocent' and 'naive'.

> ### Key quotation
>
> ...I thought long after I laid me down, how common Estella would consider Joe, a mere blacksmith: how thick his boots, and how coarse his hands.
>
> (Chapter 9, p. 72)

> ### Key quotation
>
> Pip explains to Biddy: 'The beautiful young lady at Miss Havisham's, and she's more beautiful than anybody ever was, and I admire her dreadfully, and I want to be a gentleman on her account.'
>
> (Chapter 17, p. 129)

> ### Key quotation
>
> We spent as much money as we could, and got as little for it as people could make up their minds to give us. We were always more or less miserable...
>
> (Chapter 34, p. 274)

founded on the wealth of an ex-convict. As a result, his social standing is invalid in the eyes of the snobbish upper-class world to which he has aspired. Furthermore, Pip now realises that his wealth does not derive from Miss Havisham, as he had mistakenly believed. Pip the narrator explains how it has become apparent to his younger self that his hopes have all been 'a mere dream; Estella not designed for me...' (Chapter 39, p. 323). The immediate realisation which follows, now that the illusion has been dispelled, is that of his own 'worthless conduct' towards Joe and Biddy (Chapter 39, p. 323).

The return of this instinctive sense of right and wrong, which Pip had possessed as a child, becomes the guiding principle that steers him through Volume III, the concluding part of the novel. Pip shows compassion and affection towards the ex-convict Magwitch, secretly ensures that Herbert's fortunes are advanced, generously forgives Miss Havisham for the misery she has caused him, and reconciles himself to both Joe and Biddy, whom he now views with the respect that their upright characters so clearly deserve.

His reward for the painful spiritual journey that he has undertaken during the course of the novel is his ultimate union with his heart's desire — Estella — but not the unfeeling damaged child of Satis House. He is to be accompanied through the rest of his life by a mature woman who, through her own painful progress, has now learnt the innate value of the unconditional love that Pip has long offered. As she openly declares herself, it is a love that she had once 'thrown away when...quite ignorant of its worth' (Chapter 59, p. 484). The journey that Pip has shared with the reader illustrates the novel's essential moral theme — that it is the quality of the individual that really counts, not the eminence of their social position.

Estella

- adopted and educated by Miss Havisham to break men's hearts
- beautiful
- proud and arrogant
- indifferent to her own fate and that of others
- under the direction of Miss Havisham for most of the novel
- eventually breaks free from Miss Havisham's control but only to make a disastrous marriage to Bentley Drummle
- exhibits emotional and spiritual growth as a result of her own pain and suffering
- ultimately comes to recognise the value of such powerful and positive emotions as love, forgiveness and remorse

Estella is the heroine of *Great Expectations*. She is one of the few characters who is never mocked by Dickens' ironic narrative voice. As a result, there is a genuine element of tragedy about Estella, which arises from her status as the victim of Miss Havisham's obsessive and pathological desire for vengeance. Estella, the natural daughter of Magwitch and Molly, was adopted by Miss Havisham at the age of three in order to become a weapon against men.

By this point in the novel, Herbert's assessment of Estella's character has been well confirmed to the reader by her previous behaviour towards Pip. When the two meet as children she treats him with condescension, contempt and cruelty. At their first encounter, she insolently demands to know 'Why don't you cry?' (Chapter 8, p. 65). At their second meeting, the mature Pip narrates that 'she slapped my face with such force as she had' (Chapter 11, p. 82), seemingly to prove that she is consistently insulting.

She then disappears from Pip's life for an unspecified period of years. While Pip has become Joe's apprentice, Miss Havisham triumphantly declares that Estella has been sent

Estella and Pip.

Key quotation

'That girl's hard and haughty and capricious to the last degree, and has been brought up by Miss Havisham to wreak revenge on all the male sex.'
(Chapter 22, p. 177)

'Abroad…educating for a lady; far out of reach; prettier than ever; admired by all who see her.'

(Chapter 15, p. 116)

Miss Havisham's cruel assertion that Estella is far beyond Pip's grasp may also provide the reader with a clue to the charactonym of her name: Estella means star-like. This deliberate symbolism is reinforced during Pip's first visit to Satis House when Pip the narrator describes how 'her light came along the long dark passage like a star' (Chapter 8, p. 59). The image is continued when Pip describes how it was 'as if she were going out into the sky' (Chapter 8, p. 64).

On her return from France as a young lady of approximately 20, there appears to be a marked improvement in Estella's demeanour. Her manners and behaviour are now those of an apparently sophisticated young lady rather than those of a spiteful and spoilt child. On meeting her again at Satis House, Pip the narrator comments on how Estella was

Key quotation

'Oh! I have a heart to be stabbed in or shot in, I have no doubt,' said Estella, 'and, of course, if it ceased to beat I should cease to be. But you know what I mean. I have no softness there, no — sympathy — sentiment — nonsense.'
(Chapter 29, p. 237)

Key quotation

'...suffering has been stronger than all other teaching, and has taught me to understand what your heart used to be. I have been bent and broken, but — I hope — into a better shape.'

(Chapter, 59, p. 484)

Pause for thought

Again, notice the different ways in which Dickens reveals character: Estella's actions, Estella's remarks about herself, Herbert's observations, the narrator's observations and Dickens' use of imagery. Why do you think Dickens reveals evidence about his characters through a variety of means?

Miss Havisham

- wealthy heiress and inheritor of a brewery business which she has allowed to fall into disuse
- locked in a time warp stemming from the exact moment at which she was jilted at the altar by Compeyson on her birthday
- reclusive and lives in a virtual prison of her own making
- fundamentally motivated by her desire 'to wreak revenge on all the male sex'
- egocentric and incapable of empathy until near the end of her life
- mentally ill and most likely anorexic

Grade *booster*

The most appropriate definition for the way irony has been used here would be 'contradiction'.

Key quotation

...she had the appearance of having dropped, body and soul, within and without, under the weight of a crushing blow.

(Chapter 8, p. 61)

Miss Havisham's name may be symbolic, being a compound of the verb 'have' and the noun 'sham', meaning something false. The irony of 'having' fits in well with the name of her mansion, Satis House — *satis* being Latin for 'enough'. Materially, Miss Havisham can have anything she wants, but spiritually she is clearly impoverished. Through his characterisation, Dickens demonstrates to the reader an essential moral message/theme — wealth is not enough, and without love, money is not worth having.

Blinded by hate, Miss Havisham wilfully chooses to live in the moment of the greatest crisis of her life, that being twenty minutes to nine on an unspecified birthday sometime in the past when Compeyson cruelly jilted her. This is signalled by a number of facts: all of her clocks have been stopped at this time, she still wears her now heavily decaying wedding dress, and the wedding table remains set with a rotting wedding cake at its centre.

Her physical appearance at various times in the novel is denoted by such words as 'skeleton' (Chapter 8, p. 58), 'corpse-like' (Chapter 8, p. 60), 'grave-clothes' (Chapter 8, p. 60) and 'spectre' (Chapter 17, p. 125). The impression is of an under-nourished recluse whose only release from her insanity will be death. Her emaciation may well be as a result of an eating disorder to which Jaggers refers when, as Pip the narrator recalls, 'he asked me how often I had seen Miss Havisham eat and drink...' (Chapter 29, p. 241).

Miss Havisham.

ITV/Rex Features

Pause for thought

Trace the use of food and feasting throughout the novel. What kinds of characters are shown in the act of eating? How does Dickens use food to reveal character? Look, for example, at the Christmas feast in Chapter 4 and the theft of the pork pie for Magwitch in Chapters 2 and 3.

Dickens subtly develops the connection between Miss Havisham, food and death in a variety ways. On the table where the uneaten wedding cake decays (uneaten, that is, apart from the gnawing of hungry mice), Miss Havisham expects to be laid out when dead (Chapter 11, p. 89). On the previous page (Chapter 11, p. 88) she envisages her grasping relatives 'come to feast upon me' once she is dead. And much later in the novel, Dickens extends the metaphor when he has Pip the narrator describe Miss Havisham's desperate admiration of Estella as being as if 'she were devouring the beautiful creature she had reared' (Chapter 38, p. 302).

This pattern of cannibalistic imagery powerfully associates Miss Havisham's psychological and spiritual starvation with Compeyson's cynical rejection of her on her wedding day. It also links this rejection with her equally cynical exploitation of Estella. Furthermore, it helps to portray Miss Havisham as another genuinely tragic figure who, like Estella, is spared the comic mocking narrative tone to which so many of the other characters are subjected.

Dickens underlines both the physical and spiritual deterioration of Miss Havisham in his characterisation of Satis House. The once thriving brewery has now fallen into disuse and both the grounds and buildings are heavily neglected. Pip the narrator portrays it as a 'dismal' property which is 'rustily barred' (Chapter 8, p. 55) and has a 'rank garden' full of 'tangled weeds' (Chapter 8, p. 64).

Grade *booster*

A metaphor is a comparison in which one thing is said to be literally another thing, *or* when one thing is said to be able to do something which it literally cannot do. Miss Havisham's relatives will not literally 'feast' upon her corpse.

Grade *booster*

There are various reasons why a writer might use such a figure of speech but, in general, metaphors enable a writer to create a clearer and more vivid picture of the original thing that is being described to the reader. Metaphors can also make the writing more poetic, humorous or dramatic.

Again, the imagery used here is intentional. The frequent references to 'wilderness' and 'weeds' are emblematic of the great 'fall' and consequent moral corruption of Miss Havisham. There is a biblical echo here of Adam and Eve who were also corrupted and fell from grace, ultimately being expelled from the Garden of Eden to the wilderness beyond. The frequent references to bars suggest the way in which Miss Havisham has made herself a prisoner of the painful rejection that she cannot overcome.

It is only while close to death and, as she prophesied, when laid out on her bridal table, that she is finally able to comprehend the extent of the harm that she has inflicted on both Pip and Estella. Her last words to Pip are an impassioned plea for forgiveness (Chapter 49, p. 403).

Grade *booster*

Imagery refers to the use of such techniques as metaphors and similes. An imagery pattern is when an image is repeatedly used within a text in order to reinforce an impression of someone or something. Examiners are impressed if you are able to write about stylistic features.

Text *focus*

Read the description of Miss Havisham on page 60 (Chapter 8) from 'It was then I began to understand...' to '...would have struck her to dust'. Compare this with the description of the wedding dining room in Satis House on page 84 (Chapter 11): 'I crossed the staircase landing...transpired in the spider community'. Compare the two extracts and consider how many parallels Dickens has intentionally created between Miss Havisham and her house.

Abel Magwitch

- Pip's mysterious benefactor
- victim of both society and Compeyson
- common law husband of Molly, Jaggers' maid
- transported for life to Australia
- becomes a wealthy sheep farmer and stock breeder
- Estella's real father, though this is not revealed until late in the novel

---

Grade *booster*

An analogy is a similarity.

Magwitch's first name, Abel, is another example of Dickens' use of charactonym. Although Magwitch may look like a desperate murderer at various points in the novel, his forename identifies him as a victim as opposed to a slayer. Cain and Abel were sons of Adam and Eve, and it was Cain who committed the first ever murder when he killed his brother. The biblical Abel is also a shepherd, which further strengthens the analogy. The religious symbolism inherent in this name ties in well with Dickens' deliberate use of the marshes to reflect the hostile world to which Adam and Eve (and all mankind) are expelled after their rebellion against God. This is the morally flawed fallen world that humanity has inherited. Hence the references in Chapter 5 to a 'dismal wilderness' with its 'wicked Noah's ark'.

Magwitch is another of the limited number of characters in *Great Expectations* who grow through time. He is crucial to the development of the plot as he is the unnamed benefactor behind Pip's sudden change in circumstances. Furthermore, because he insists on secrecy, Magwitch's structural role in the novel is to enable both Pip and the reader to be misled into assuming Miss Havisham is the benefactor and, more importantly, that Miss Havisham has ultimately destined Pip to be betrothed to Estella. As well as helping to drive the action of the entire novel, Magwitch also provides much of the tension and suspense that engage the reader's interest in the opening chapters.

On his first appearance, Magwitch is a desperate figure prepared to cut the throat of a young child (Chapter 1, p. 4). However, Dickens subtly maintains sympathy for him by referring to his hunger, his various wounds and his uncontrollable shivering. His second meeting with Pip (Chapter 3, p. 19) reveals a gentle and more gracious nature as he politely thanks Pip for the food. However, his violent struggle with Compeyson (Chapter 5, p. 36) reminds us that this is a dangerous man.

Magwitch is soon transported to Australia for the various crimes he committed with Compeyson and, once there, makes a fortune. However, he risks all some 16 years later to return to England to reveal himself as Pip's true benefactor. The reader's first impression of him at this point is not favourable. Dickens purposefully reminds us of his violent past by the fact that he frequently brandishes a knife and also utters such threatening statements as 'don't catch hold of me. You'd be sorry arterwards...' (Chapter 39, p. 315). However, the most disturbing aspect of his character is his sense of proprietorship over Pip: 'If I ain't a gentleman...I'm the owner of such' (Chapter 39, p. 321). It is also clear that his motives for advancing Pip are essentially self-serving and are bound up in his desire to assert his supremacy over an established order which has previously made him feel powerless and inferior.

It is not long, though, before Dickens tones down these initial blusters of arrogance and bravado to reveal a man who has greatly mellowed as a result of the hardships of his life. As Herbert remarks to Pip, 'I thought he was softened when I last saw him' (Chapter 50, p. 405).

> ### Key quotation
>
> '...blast you every one, from the judge in his wig, to the colonist a stirring up the dust, I'll show a better gentleman than the whole kit on you put together!'
> (Chapter 40, p. 332)

Text focus

Read Magwitch's account of his early life on pp. 346–47 (Chapter 42), beginning 'Dear boy and Pip's comrade...' and ending '...wore out my good share of key-metal still'. Consider the various ways in which society has failed Magwitch and thus driven him to crime.

His reasons for making Pip a gentleman are also revised in a way that creates compassion for Magwitch. It becomes clear that he was moved by the young Pip's loyalty towards him and that Pip's sincerity rekindled the love that he felt for his own lost daughter whom he still believes to be dead.

Magwitch gains most sympathy at the end of the novel, when he is once again betrayed by the villain Compeyson just as he is on the point of escaping to safety. The severe injuries that he sustains while avenging himself on Compeyson, and his harsh treatment by a judicial system which would prefer to hang him before he can die of his life-threatening injuries, ensure his full rehabilitation in the eyes of the reader. Magwitch represents the theme of the essential goodness of a common man despite all of the social disadvantages that he has faced in life. Dickens has clearly designed him as a deliberate contrast to the corrupt and immoral behaviour of such social 'superiors' as Compeyson and Miss Havisham.

Magwitch is also crucial in Pip's rehabilitation. Pip's compassion and recognition of Magwitch's worth as a human being finally put an end to the superficial snobbery which have beset him since he became a gentleman. By the end, not only is Pip able to appreciate Magwitch's humanity, he has also learnt to appreciate the moral superiority of Joe and Biddy and, hence, his own shameful ingratitude towards them.

> ### Key quotation
>
> ...he pondered over the question whether he might have been a better man under better circumstances. But, he never justified himself by a hint tending that way, or tried to bend the past out of its eternal shape.
>
> (Chapter 56, p. 456)

Grade *focus*

How will you be assessed on character-based questions?

Higher grades: A*–C
Answers will show perceptive insight into the nature of characters and the author's methods for revealing aspects of character to the reader. There will also be a clear appreciation that characters are constructs designed by the author and are often used to represent themes and ideas as well as being believable creations. Evidence will be carefully selected and thoughtfully evaluated.

Lower grades: D–G
Candidates will tend to discuss characters as if they are real people.

Review your learning

(Answers on p. 91)
1. What five methods does Charles Dickens use to reveal his characters?
2. What does 'charactonym' mean?
3. Which of the characters reviewed in this section develop or change?
4. What changes take place in Pip during the course of the novel?
5. In what ways are Miss Havisham and Estella the victims of others?
6. What theme or idea does Magwitch represent?

More interactive questions and answers online.

Themes

- What is a theme?
- What are the main themes in *Great Expectations*?
- How do these themes relate to each other?
- How do these themes relate to the characters?

A theme in a novel is an idea that the author explores through such means as character, plot and language. In Dickens' case, the themes that he examines are usually in order to instruct the reader on a moral point and, consequently, there is bound to be some overlap between them. Here is a list of some important themes in Great Expectations:

- gentility and social class
- education
- justice and mercy
- romantic love
- forgiveness and redemption

Gentility and social class

One of the most important themes in Great Expectations is that of social status and, in particular, what it means to be a gentleman — or a lady. The lust after greater status is established in the second chapter with the entrance of Mrs Joe who caustically comments, 'It's bad enough to be a blacksmith's wife (and him a Gargery) without being your mother' (Chapter 2, p. 9). This is a preoccupation with Mrs Joe and recurs again in Chapter 4 when she laments, 'Perhaps if I warn't a blacksmith's wife…' (p. 22). In fact, it is through her equally snobbish and aspiring Uncle Pumblechook that the connection with Miss Havisham is first made. As these are two equally unpleasant characters, it is immediately clear that Dickens is condemning such social aspirations. Mrs Joe and Pumblechook are essentially self-seeking and self-serving individuals and, therefore, any rise in their status would not be used for the general good.

Pip's introduction to the supposedly genteel world of Satis House is a most unpleasant experience. Gentility is demonstrated to be little more than an excuse to belittle those with lesser fortunes and status. It is explicitly associated with materialism, snobbery, vanity, cruelty, superficiality and injustice. This is evidently a lesson that Miss Havisham has

Grade *booster*

Although the exam boards tend to set questions on either themes or characters, it is important to realise that this division is artificial. Characters are one method by which an author develops themes.

Key quotation

I took the opportunity of being alone in the court-yard, to look at my coarse hands and my common boots. My opinion of those accessories was not favourable. They had never troubled me before, but they troubled me now, as vulgar appendages. I determined to ask Joe why he had ever taught me to call those picture-cards, Jacks, which ought to be called knaves. I wished Joe had been rather more genteelly brought up, and then I should have been so too.

(Chapter 8, p. 62)

taught Estella. With Miss Havisham's approval Estella instantly sets about humiliating Pip, calling him 'a common labouring-boy' and complaining that 'He calls the knaves, Jacks' (Chapter 8, p. 60). Pip is then reminded of his place in society when Miss Havisham instructs Estella to 'Let him have something to eat' (Chapter 8, p. 62) exactly as though he were a servant. The result of this experience is Pip's distress and the start of his unsettling feelings of inadequacy and dissatisfaction with his position in life.

It is, of course, such superficial qualities of gentility as appearance and vocabulary that have been impressed upon him rather than anything solid or worthwhile. When Pip describes Estella to Biddy, Dickens is able to offer a more mature and considered viewpoint. Biddy's opinion is that if Pip's aspiration to be a gentleman is because he wishes to 'gain' Estella then 'she was not worth gaining over' (Chapter 17, p. 129). The narrator confirms the validity of Biddy's conclusion by stating 'Biddy was the wisest of girls...' (Chapter 17, p. 129). Biddy offers further insights on the topic of gentility when she remarks 'a gentleman should not be unjust neither...' (Chapter 19, p. 150).

Herbert and Matthew Pocket are two more characters whose opinions the reader is encouraged to value and they also offer insights into what being a gentleman should mean.

The reason why Pip aspires to a higher social stratum is in order to obtain the morally inferior but captivatingly beautiful Estella. Once Pip finally attains the status that he so desires, Estella remains beyond his reach and the world of a gentleman is shown to be a shallow and pointless existence which only leads to debt and moral degradation. (For a fuller analysis of this point, see the character study of Pip on pp. 29–32 of this guide.)

However, as Dickens demonstrates through his characterisation of tradespeople such as Trabb, society values money and status rather than innate nobility: 'So, Mr. Trabb measured and calculated me, in the parlour, as if I were an estate...' (Chapter 19, p. 152). This simile makes Trabb's materialism explicit — Pip is quite clearly regarded as a valuable property to be exploited rather than as a human being.

Other characters who exemplify the futile and redundant lifestyle of the gentleman include the Finches, of whom the narrator remarks that they

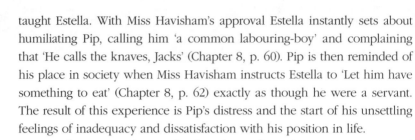

Key quotation

Herbert, quoting his father, tells Pip: '...no man who was not a true gentleman at heart, ever was, since the world began, a true gentleman in manner.'

(Chapter 22, p. 181)

Grade *booster*

A simile is a comparison in which one thing is said to be 'like' or 'as' another thing. Writers use similes (and metaphors) in order to create a clearer and more vivid (visual) impression of the original thing that they are trying to describe to the reader.

ITV/Rex Features

Pip the gentleman.

'spent their money foolishly...' (Chapter 34, p. 273). The most degenerate member of the Finches club is, without doubt, Bentley Drummle. As we are informed in Chapter 23 (p. 192), he is 'the next heir but one to a baronetcy'. The narrator also describes him as 'idle, proud, niggardly, reserved, and suspicious' (Chapter 25, p. 203). Furthermore, he is 'Heavy in figure, movement, and comprehension...' and, as the narrator ironically remarks, '... took up a book as if its writer had done him an injury...' (Chapter 25, pp. 202–03). His marriage to Estella is everything one would expect of such a dubious moral character.

Another character that Dickens uses to expose the contradiction that often exists between gentility of rank and gentility of nature is the villainous Compeyson. Despite social status and education, Compeyson is the primary example of a villain in the novel and the one person most responsible, either directly or indirectly, for the various evils that beset most of the main characters. He jilts Miss Havisham on her wedding day, thus initiating her heartbreak and her obsessive desire for revenge on all men. This quite clearly has a major negative impact on the lives of both Pip and Estella. He also uses his knowledge of Magwitch's personal circumstances with regard to Molly and her supposed murder of their child in order to blackmail Magwitch into participating in his criminal schemes. When Herbert relates this aspect of Magwitch's history to Pip, he refers to 'That evil genius, Compeyson, the worst of scoundrels among many scoundrels...' (Chapter 50, p. 407). It is also Compeyson who twice betrays Magwitch, the second occasion leading to Magwitch's recapture and ultimate death just as he is on the point of escaping the country (Chapter 54).

Education

It is clear from the above section on gentility that the education provided for the upper classes was often lacking in any real value. It certainly seems to have had no positive impact on either Compeyson or Drummle. Estella, also, has been sent 'Abroad...educating for a lady...' (Chapter 15, p. 116). On her return many years later, all she seems to have learnt is how to ensnare men.

Another damning indictment of the education system provided for upper-class women is the example of Mrs Pocket, Matthew Pocket's hopelessly disorganised and inefficient wife. Her father was a Knight and had her educated as befitted the family's elevated social position. It is clear that being socially useful or personally sufficient is not regarded as a relevant skill. And, again, emphasis is primarily placed on such superficial features as appearance.

Key quotation

I had heard of her as leading a most unhappy life, and as being separated from her husband, who had used her with great cruelty, and who had become quite renowned as a compound of pride, avarice, brutality, and meanness.
(Chapter 59, p. 482)

Key quotation

'He set up fur a gentleman, this Compeyson, and he'd been to a public boarding-school and had learning. He was a smooth one to talk, and was a dab at the ways of gentlefolks.'
(Chapter 42, p. 347)

Grade *booster*

You will help to improve your grade by demonstrating to your examiner an understanding that themes do not appear in isolation but are interwoven and inter-connected. The power of their combination is to reinforce the overall intellectual or moral message of the novel.

Be that as it may, he had directed Mrs. Pocket to be brought up from her cradle as one who in the nature of things must marry a title, and who was to be guarded from the acquisition of plebeian domestic knowledge. So successful a watch and ward had been established over the young lady by this judicious parent, that she had grown up highly ornamental, but perfectly helpless and useless.

(Chapter 23, p. 189)

Despite the dubious nature of the education provided for the privileged, Dickens makes it abundantly clear that, as far as the rich and powerful are concerned, a good education is to remain beyond the reach of the lower classes. As Pip the narrator comments in Chapter 12 (p. 95), Miss Havisham '…seemed to prefer my being ignorant'. The reason for this, though not given at this point in the novel, is because education fosters talent and encourages a meritocracy, a society where people rise through ability, as opposed to an aristocracy where those who hold power and wealth do so through no other reason than the good fortune of their birth. As Herbert explains to Pip in Chapter 22, Miss Havisham's father 'was a country gentleman down in your part of the world, and was a brewer' (p. 180). However, Miss Havisham, who 'was a spoilt child' (p. 180), has allowed the highly successful brewery business to fall idle and has entirely adopted the unproductive lifestyle which Dickens more regularly associated with her class. It is Joe who sums up the real power of education when, commenting on Mrs Joe, he remarks:

'And she an't over partial to having scholars on the premises,' Joe continued, 'and in partickler would not be over partial to my being a scholar, for fear as I might rise. Like a sort of rebel, don't you see?'

(Chapter 7, p. 49)

Consequently, the quality of education that is available to the poor is generally intentionally substandard. Certainly, both Joe and Magwitch are clear evidence of the lack of a worthwhile educational provision for those less well off.

Text focus

Read the description of the school run for the local children by Mr Wopsle's great-aunt in Chapter 10 (pp. 73–74), which begins 'The Educational scheme or Course' and ends 'one low-spirited dip-candle and no snuffers'. Consider the various ways in which Dickens presents this as being a poor quality of schooling.

Education is not just an isolated social theme that Dickens chooses to explore within the novel. It also becomes a key aspect of Pip's own character development. As a result of his first contact with Estella and Miss

Havisham, Pip perceives education as a means to upward social mobility, most likely reflecting Dickens' own social advancement through academic means. As Pip the narrator states at the beginning of Chapter 10:

> …I had a particular reason for wishing to get on in life, and that I should feel very much obliged to her if she would impart all her learning to me.
>
> (p. 73)

Of course, once he is to become a gentleman, a more formal education is seen as an essential prerequisite. As Jaggers remarks when he informs Pip of his good fortune, 'It is considered that you must be better educated, in accordance with your altered position…' (Chapter 18, p. 139). Admittedly this education does have its frivolous aspects, as Herbert indicates when he explains, on Pip's first night in London, the vital importance of using a fork and not holding a spoon 'over-hand' (Chapter 22, p. 179). However, because Jaggers is a man of good sense, he ensures that Pip's London tutor, Matthew Pocket, is an able instructor. And, ultimately, it is not Pip's temporary existence as Magwitch's idle and artificially manufactured gentleman that secures his future, but his education, which enables him to become a productive and industrious partner in Clarriker's business where 'we had a good name, and worked for our profits, and did very well' (Chapter 58, p. 480).

Justice and mercy

In the novels of Charles Dickens, justice and mercy are crucially important themes which often drive the plot forward. Much of the sense of outrage and anger that Dickens communicates to the reader is created by a failure of natural justice on the part of the law and an absence of mercy on the part of those who hold power.

In *Great Expectations*, as in many of Dickens' other works, the law is unjust and unequal, favouring the small, powerful and monied elite at the top of society. Admittedly, Jaggers is treated with great respect and Wemmick with an equal amount of affection. In Chapter 18, for example, Jaggers expounds upon the finer ideals of his profession when he demands of Wopsle whether or not he is aware of the fact that:

> '…the law of England supposes every man to be innocent, until he is proved — proved — to be guilty?'
>
> (p. 134)

However, there is also a wider world of legal indifference, incompetence and corruption which prevails just beyond Jaggers' office. The young Pip is aware of the law as a tool of oppression of the lower classes. After

---

Grade *booster*

An examiner will be impressed if you are able to demonstrate a brief and relevant understanding of how key events in a writer's life have influenced his or her work. In order to read about the crucial importance of education in Dickens' own life, see p. 7 of this guide.

Pause for thought

Having considered the importance of education within the novel, how does it make you feel about your own right to a free place in a state school? How might a modern reader's opinion on this subject differ from a Victorian reader's opinion?

Grade *booster*

Think about how Dickens uses the theme of justice and mercy as a plot device. He uses it to deepen the reader's emotional attachment to his heroes and heroines while simultaneously critiquing one of the great evils of his society.

his impromptu boxing bout with the youthful Herbert Pocket, his thoughts are conveyed as:

> …the Law would avenge it. Without having any definite idea of the penalties I had incurred, it was clear to me that village boys could not go stalking about the country, ravaging the houses of gentlefolks and pitching into the studious youth of England, without laying themselves open to severe punishment.
>
> (Chapter 12, pp. 93–94)

But the person who most suffers as a result of the class discrimination at the heart of the legal system is, of course, Magwitch. Shortly after his revelation that he is Pip's benefactor, he relates the events that caused him to become the escaped convict whom Pip helped on the momentous day described at the opening of the novel. Both Magwitch and Compeyson had been arrested for what would be termed today as money-laundering, 'a charge of putting stolen notes in circulation…' (Chapter 42, p. 350). However, although Magwitch was the junior partner in the crime, he was given the lion's share of the sentence. Magwitch explains:

> 'And when it come to character, warn't it Compeyson as had been to the school, and warn't it his schoolfellows as was in this position and in that, and warn't it him as had been know'd by witnesses in such clubs and societies, and nowt to his disadvantage?'
>
> (Chapter 42, p. 351)

The heavily biased and unfair verdict is that Compeyson receives a sentence of seven years whereas Magwitch's term is set at fourteen years. The tragic conclusion to Magwitch's role within the novel again points out the heartlessness of the system. The judge sentences Magwitch to hang rather than mercifully delaying the sentence so that he can be left to die of his injuries. The brutality of the system is also highlighted by the fact that on the day appointed for Magwitch's execution, he will be just one of a total of 'two-and-thirty men and women' sentenced to death (Chapter 56, p. 457).

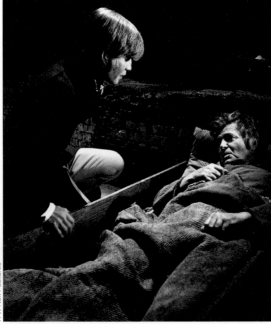

Pip comforts the dying Magwitch.

Romantic love

Great Expectations is one of Dickens' most romantic novels, most likely because of his relationship with the young actress Ellen Ternan (see pp. 7–8 of this guide). As well as being a major theme, Pip's unrequited love for Estella is essential to the overall structure of the novel as it helps to drive the plot forward. As in all romances, the main source of suspense is the reader's curiosity as to how, and even *if*, the problem that separates the potential lovers will be resolved.

In the original ending to the novel, Dickens had Estella marry a 'Shropshire doctor' after the death of Drummle. Before publication, Dickens showed this ending to Sir Edward Bulwer-Lytton, a friend and fellow-novelist, who strongly urged him to write a more positive conclusion so as not to disappoint the reader. On the basis of this advice, Dickens decided to change the ending to what we now have, a strong implication of a future marriage between Pip and Estella some time after the novel ends.

A perfect example of ideal romantic love within the novel is Herbert Pocket's relationship with Clara Barley. It is never sufficiently developed to be termed a subplot, but it does act as a dramatic contrast to Pip's relationship with Estella and allows Dickens to offer observations concerning the true nature of romantic love. Herbert intends to marry Clara regardless of the fact that 'she is rather below my mother's nonsensical family notions' (Chapter 30, p. 252). It is her character and not her social status that is her defining quality. Pip as narrator later describes her as having 'something so confiding, loving, and innocent, in her modest manner of yielding herself to Herbert's embracing arm...' (Chapter 46, p. 376). Estella, by contrast, is incapable of love at this time in her life owing to Miss Havisham's training, and so Herbert's match with Clara starkly contrasts with Estella's own socially desirable but essentially frigid and violent union with Drummle.

The darker side of romantic love is explored through Miss Havisham. Her definition of love is savagely imparted to Pip when he visits Satis House on Estella's return from her foreign education:

> 'I'll tell you,' said she, in the same hurried passionate whisper, 'what real love is. It is blind devotion, unquestioning self-humiliation, utter submission, trust and belief against yourself and against the whole world, giving up your whole heart and soul to the smiter — as I did!'
>
> (Chapter 29, p. 240)

In many respects, it mirrors Pip's own obsessive and unrequited feelings for Estella. However, the main clue to the distinctive feature that distinguishes Pip's infatuation from Miss Havisham's is the use of the word 'smiter'. Her passion also embodies a powerful sense of accusation and hatred.

Forgiveness and redemption

In opposition to the increasingly secular mood of the times (see pp. 9–10 of this guide), it is clear that Dickens writes from a strongly Christian

Grade *booster*

Notice how many themes Miss Havisham encompasses: vengeance, unrequited love, upper-class indolence, adult corruption of youth, et cetera. She is an excellent example of how themes are interconnected and of how theme and character are often indivisible.

point of view and that a belief in traditional Christian values is often the motivating force behind many of the themes that he chooses to explore through his characters and plots. Towards the end of Chapter 56 (p. 458), for example, the narrator refers to 'the greater Judgment that knoweth all things and cannot err'. Forgiveness and redemption are two Christian virtues that feature prominently in *Great Expectations*.

The novel undoubtedly incorporates characters who are beyond these high Christian ideals. True villains, such as Drummle, Orlick and Compeyson, never waver from their evil path. However, a number of other characters, including, of course, Pip and Magwitch, do ultimately appreciate the errors of their ways and seek to reform. This is generally associated with a strong desire for forgiveness. (For a fuller analysis of both Pip and Magwitch, see the relevant parts of the *Characterisation* section in this guide.)

For characters such as Miss Havisham, Mrs Joe and Arthur (Miss Havisham's deceitful half-brother), their moral epiphany (awakening) comes late and, therefore, they are unable to reap the kind of spiritual and psychological benefits of living with a clear conscience that enrich Pip's life at the latter stages of the novel. However, in each of the above cases, shortly before their deaths, all three obtain a degree of enlightenment. The severely disabled Mrs Joe, for example, seeks Pip's forgiveness for the harsh and unloving regime of punishment that she had inflicted on him when he was a child, her last words being 'Pardon' and 'Pip' (Chapter 35, p. 283).

A much more significant exploration of these themes occurs, once again, via Miss Havisham. Her first pangs of conscience arise just before Estella drops the bombshell that she is to marry Drummle. When Miss Havisham suddenly perceives the degree of heartbreak that she has wilfully inflicted on Pip, the narrator describes seeing her 'put her hand to her heart and hold it there…' (Chapter 44, p. 362). One of the most compelling examples of both forgiveness and redemption within the entire novel occurs several chapters later between the same two characters.

It is clear from this section of their dialogue that personal reflection and self-awareness are essential prerequisites for forgiveness, which is probably why other characters make no moral improvement. Compeyson regrets nothing, including his cruel deception of Miss Havisham, but awareness of the responsibility for his role in the ruin of Miss Havisham's life haunts her half-brother Arthur to the very end. He dies as a hopeless alcoholic haunted by a vision of a heartbroken Miss Havisham.

> **Key quotation**
>
> 'My name is on the first leaf. If you can ever write under my name, "I forgive her," though ever so long after my broken heart is dust — pray do it!'
>
> 'O Miss Havisham,' said I, 'I can do it now. There have been sore mistakes; and my life has been a blind and thankless one; and I want forgiveness and direction far too much, to be bitter with you.'
>
> (Chapter 49, p. 398)

Grade *focus*

How will you be assessed on theme-based questions?

For grades A*–C, you need to do more than merely identifying themes. You should explain what techniques Dickens uses to present these themes within the novel and what impact this presentation of theme will have on readers. For example, in what ways does Dickens present the brutality of the legal system and how might this make the reader feel towards capital punishment?

Review your learning

(Answers on p. 92)

1. Which themes have been identified in this section of the guide?
2. What can we learn about Victorian society from Dickens' treatment of the themes highlighted in this section of the guide?
3. Which of these themes help Dickens to create his characters and develop his plot?
4. Which character is least identified with the theme of forgiveness?
5. Which themes are most closely associated with Dickens' own personal experiences?
6. Which characters are most identified with the theme of remorse immediately prior to their deaths?

More interactive questions and answers online.

Style

- What features does the term 'style' refer to?
- What viewpoint does Charles Dickens adopt?
- What is characteristic about Dickens' style?
- How does Dickens create humour?
- How does Dickens use settings in order to develop major themes?
- In what ways does Dickens use imagery?

Pause for thought

Think about an author whom you have enjoyed reading. In what ways are his/her novels different from or better than those of authors whom you do not like? As you consider this question, you are considering their 'style'.

Grade booster

Demonstrating an appreciation of an author's style is a sophisticated skill and exam questions are unlikely to address just this aspect. However, if you find relevant opportunities to write about style in the exam, you will be showing the examiner that your grasp of the novel is mature.

Pause for thought

In order to appreciate how unreliable a first-person narrator can be, ask yourself how much sympathy there would have been for Pip in the early chapters of the novel if the narrative had been relayed through Mrs Joe.

A definition of style

To respond to a question about 'Dickens' style', you should firstly define your terms, i.e. explain to the examiner that you understand what this phrase means in relation to this novel. A novelist's style is his or her distinctive manner of writing, i.e. what makes his or her writing unique. A writer's style may develop and change over time but will nevertheless retain characteristic features that a regular reader of that author will come to recognise.

Dickens has a distinctive style that makes his writing different from most of the novels that we would read today. His writing is also different from that of many of the authors of his own day, including Thomas Hardy, George Eliot and Elizabeth Gaskell. They tended to create characters and situations that closely resembled reality and, therefore, their style is naturalistic. Dickens also commented on real life, but tended to exaggerate characters and situations for either comic or tragic effect.

Narrative viewpoint

The first-person narrator

A major consideration when analysing style is the position from which the author writes the story. *Great Expectations* is related from the first-person narrative point of view (I), and the reader is intended to assume that the story is being told by Pip, the main character in the novel. All the perceptions and judgements in the novel are presented as being from Pip's point of view and, as he is just one character in the novel, his version of the 'truth' is just one of many possible versions.

Dickens' mocking narrative tone

'Tone' refers to the emotional feel of the writing: for example, comic, sad, angry or ironic. The tone may also be a more sophisticated combination of a number of emotions. Although *Great Expectations* is presented via a first-person narrator (Pip), much of its tone is that of the acerbic voice of Dickens himself. The bitingly ironic and often cynical voice is one of the predominant characteristics of his style, whether the novel be in the first person or in the god-like, all-knowing, omniscient third-person narrative style. It is the voice of an often judgemental narrator who cannot resist the urge to lampoon his own creations for comic effect. Even some of Dickens' most admirable characters cannot escape this heavily mocking commentary of riotous slapstick humour and are often treated in a most undignified manner.

Irony

The meaning of 'irony', as the word has been used above, is similar to sarcasm, but it is a much higher form of wit. It is when the literal sense of the writing suggests one thing, but the context of the situation tells the reader that the writer's meaning is the opposite of what the literal meaning would suggest. Dickens regularly uses this technique. So, for example, on Joe's first visit to Pip in London, the narrator compliments Joe on his ability to return his hat to his head by describing his actions as requiring 'a constant attention, and a quickness of eye and hand, very like that exacted by wicket-keeping' (Chapter 27, p. 222). It might initially appear as if the narrator is actually praising Joe's skilfulness. In reality, the writing is ironic because the narrator is really pointing out how awkward and clumsy Joe is, so much so that he cannot even keep his hat on his head.

Authorial intrusion

On occasions, Dickens actually has the narrator acknowledge the mismatch between the innate moral goodness of a character and the ruthless way in which the narrator/Dickens has ridiculed that same character in order to create humour.

As we have seen, the narrator makes extensive fun of Joe's manners, speech and clothing during his first London visit. But this disrespectful presentation creates a disparity with the high moral value that the narrator wishes to place on Joe. Dickens tries to lessen this gap by having the narrator remark:

> Joe looked at me for a single instant with something faintly like reproach. Utterly preposterous as his cravat was, and as his collars were, I was conscious of a sort of dignity in the look.
>
> (Chapter 27, p. 222)

Grade *booster*

Understanding the difference between a first- and third-person narrator is a high-level skill. A third-person narrator is god-like and all-knowing. A first-person narrator is much more limited in perception and can only view the world of the novel from one point of view.

Grade *booster*

Lampoon means to 'send up' or to make fun of. It is another characteristic feature of Dickens' style and the examiner will be impressed if you can use the word relevantly. An understanding of such terms will help you to achieve the highest grades.

Text **focus**

Read the description of Joe on page 222 (Chapter 27), from 'I really believe Joe would have prolonged this word…' to '…heaped coals of fire on my head'. Consider the various ways in which Joe is made to look ridiculous for the reader's amusement. Look particularly at the way Dickens exaggerates the awkwardness of Joe's speech, actions and dress.

Grade **booster**

It is important to recognise that interpretation is a matter of opinion — which is why you should always back up your points with evidence.

It could be argued, of course, that Pip's often disrespectful narrative tone is simply symptomatic of the character's own immaturity at this stage in the novel. But the narrative is actually told by the mature Pip reflecting upon past events and this mature narrator, unlike his younger self, is quite able to see that Joe's extreme awkwardness 'was all my fault' (p. 222). It is also worth mentioning that the narrator's heavily ironic and comically exaggerated treatment of Joe occurs from the beginning of the novel before Pip has even met Miss Havisham and Estella, that being the point at which Pip first becomes ashamed of Joe's simple rustic ways. Furthermore, the same tone is used for many other characters within the novel and, more importantly, can be heard throughout every Dickens novel — which is why it is fair to say that it is an essential aspect of Dickens' style rather than a specific quality belonging to Pip as narrator.

Another good example of the narrative voice consciously acknowledging that the lampooning of an admirable character may have gone too far is with regard to Matthew Pocket. Matthew Pocket, Herbert Pocket's father and Pip's London tutor, is generally acknowledged to be a person of high moral worth. Even Estella tells Pip how she has heard that 'he really is disinterested, and above small jealousy and spite…' (Chapter 33, p. 266). And yet the narrative voice grossly ridicules his management of his own household, which is depicted as being comically disorganised to an unbelievable degree. Ultimately, in order to restore some semblance of dignity to the worthwhile Matthew, Dickens has the narrator remark: 'Nor, did I ever regard him as having anything ludicrous about him — or anything but what was serious, honest, and good — in his tutor communication with me' (Chapter 24, p. 197).

Text **focus**

Read the passage on page 196 (Chapter 23) which begins with the housemaid saying 'Begging your pardon, ma'am' and continues to the end of that chapter. Note the typical Dickensian exaggeration of a character's weaknesses, e.g. Mrs Pocket's inability to understand the extent of the mayhem all around her. Also note the portrayal of Mr Pocket as the long-suffering husband, a classic stock comic character even in today's television sitcoms.

You could re-read all of Chapter 23 and consider the various ways in which Matthew Pocket is comically frustrated by his wife's behaviour. Also consider the various amusing ways in which Dickens portrays this frustration, e.g. his increasingly desperate hair pulling as the chapter progresses.

PHILIP ALLAN LITERATURE GUIDE **FOR GCSE**

Exceptions to the rule

There are, however, a number of characters who are either rarely or never subjected to the narrator's intense comic ridicule. These are the more serious characters within the novel, including Miss Havisham, Estella, Biddy, Bentley Drummle, Orlick and Compeyson. Their speech and behaviour is devoid of the kind of comic eccentricities explored above. When Orlick threatens violence, for example, it is no laughing matter, as in Chapter 53 when he intends to murder Pip with a stone-hammer and then dispose of his remains in a lime-kiln.

The self-ridiculing satirical narrator

It is worth noting that Pip the character is also ridiculed by Pip the narrator. On these occasions the biting ironic tone has more of a satirical purpose, that being to show how pompous and ridiculous Pip has become as a result of his new-found status as a gentleman. An excellent example of this is the narrator's use of Trabb's boy, particularly in Chapter 30. Although only a minor character and of a low social status himself, the boy is able to see the ludicrous nature of Pip's snobbish behaviour. Therefore, he provides a stark contrast to Trabb, and the other local businessmen, who are falling over themselves to take Pip seriously because all they can see is money and rank.

Grade booster

Reminder: satire is when a writer uses humour to make a moral point by making fun of the vice or folly of someone or something.

The romantic narrative voice

There is, however, a different kind of narrative voice that surfaces significantly on occasions. Although still obviously an aspect of Dickens' style (as it is he and not Pip who has actually written the novel), this voice could be regarded as the authentic voice of Pip the character who both appears in the novel and narrates the story. In Chapter 30, while discussing Pip's relations with Estella, Herbert describes Pip as 'a boy whom nature and circumstances made so romantic...' (p. 250). When the narrative voice also becomes so romantic that it no longer embodies Dickens' characteristic sermonising or mocking tone, then this could be viewed as Pip rather than Dickens speaking.

Text focus

For a perfect example of the romantic tone of Pip's narrative voice, re-read Chapter 44, in which Pip recounts the horror and dismay he feels when his beloved Estella informs him that she is to marry the heartless and insensitive Bentley Drummle.

Compare this with the opening page of Chapter 45 when Pip has to stay overnight in a rundown hotel. The comic narrative voice returns with a sudden vengeance, this time lampooning the furniture. The bedroom, for example, is described as having 'a despotic monster of a four-post bedstead in it...' (p. 366). Consider what other aspects of this room are presented in an amusing and ironic way.

Humour

Slapstick humour

Slapstick humour is associated with physical action of a boisterous and often ridiculous nature and is a Dickensian stylistic feature. Much slapstick humour is created through the use of random acts of violence, talk about random acts of violence or the desire to commit such acts of violence. Dickens is able to turn what would be horrific in reality into amusement for the reader because of his use of caricature. In this respect his style is similar to such children's cartoons as *Bugs Bunny* and *Tom and Jerry* where the most extreme act, such as blowing somebody up or dropping them off a cliff, is funny because there is no real harm done and any pain experienced is moderate and short lived. In Dickens' time, a comparable form of entertainment would have been the *Punch and Judy* puppet shows.

An early example of this stylistic feature occurs in Chapter 2, during which Mrs Joe makes a variety of physical assaults on both the seven-year-old Pip and the adult Joe.

> By this time, my sister was quite desperate, so she pounced on Joe, and, taking him by the two whiskers, knocked his head for a little while against the wall behind him…
>
> (Chapter 2, pp. 11–12)

In the same chapter, Pip and Joe are both dosed with tar-water (a vile tasting concoction of tar and water generally used as a disinfectant) and Pip is savagely lashed with Tickler and then hurled as 'a connubial missile' (p. 9) at the hapless Joe.

Although fundamentally a gentle and good-natured character, even Pip is not immune from the desire to commit cartoon violence, as is demonstrated in Chapter 43 (p. 356), when Pip the narrator reveals that his 23-year-old self would like to take Bentley Drummle in his arms 'and seat him on the fire'.

Other comic techniques

Dickens also creates comedy through his use of such techniques as incongruity, juxtaposition, eccentric dialogue or behaviour, puns and exaggeration. The comedy often arises from the combination of any number of these techniques. The impact can be particularly hilarious when he includes slapstick humour as well.

Pause for thought

Humour, like music, is a difficult thing to explain because its effect is emotional and, therefore, irrational. When analysing a comic passage from *Great Expectations*, point out and explain the stylistic features that Dickens uses to signal humour to the reader.

Pause for thought

If these acts of violence were treated realistically by the narrator, Chapter 2 would constitute a case of severe child abuse. How would that affect the tone of the novel?

Text focus

For a good example of all aspects of Dickens' comic technique, read the Christmas dinner scene in Chapter 4. Notice the following:

- The behaviour of most of the adults is incongruous (inappropriate). They are spiteful towards Pip on an occasion which should reflect the season of goodwill.
- Pumblechook, in particular, is ludicrous (ridiculously eccentric). For example, he verbally attacks Pip by comparing him to a pig to be slaughtered by 'Dunstable the butcher' (p. 27).
- There is an example of juxtaposition when 'the Pumblechookian elbow [was] in my eye' (p. 25). Juxtaposition is the placing in close proximity of unrelated things which can then create humour through the inappropriateness of their connection.
- There is use of a pun (a double meaning) when Pumblechook tells Pip that Mrs Joe 'brought you up by hand' (p. 26). Pumblechook is using the phrase to imply that Mrs Joe's touch is caring and maternal, but the reader knows that her touch is that of frequent and unprovoked bouts of violence.
- An excellent example of slapstick humour occurs when the pompous Pumblechook drinks the adulterated brandy and displays exaggerated symptoms of distress: 'violently plunging and expectorating, making the most hideous faces, and apparently out of his mind' (p. 28).

Grade *booster*

The examiner will be impressed if you respond to a question on Dickens' creation of humour through the use of such sophisticated vocabulary as 'incongruity', 'juxtaposition', 'ludicrous', 'irony' and 'pun'.

Settings and symbolism

As you read this section, notice how settings are not just used to set the scene but are also frequently used to symbolise much bigger ideas such as the harshness of Pip's life, the frequent cruelty of humankind or the moral shortcomings of society.

The marshes

Dickens sometimes uses landscape and setting in order to represent the harshness of life. The most comprehensive way in which this meaning is conveyed in *Great Expectations* is through the depiction of the marshes which surround Pip's village. Outside Joe's forge and just beyond his warm hearth is a world of seemingly perpetual cold and mist. On the opening page of Chapter 1, the narrator immediately sets the scene when he refers to 'a memorable raw afternoon' and 'a bleak place overgrown with nettles', meaning the churchyard. The reader is introduced to an inhospitable world in which nature is both hostile and threatening. The sense of menace is further enhanced by the fact that the location is a graveyard and, judging from the high number of Pip's deceased relatives, it is a world in which death is more prevalent than life.

The sense of an antagonistic and dangerous world is further reinforced by the reference to 'a gibbet with some chains hanging to it which had once held a pirate' (Chapter 1, p. 7). A gibbet is a gallows and clearly the pirate had been publicly hung upon it. In Chapter 5, to further reinforce the point, the narrator uses pathetic fallacy and states 'the weather was cold and threatening' (p. 34). Also in Chapter 5, the narrator employs personification when he refers to 'the low red glare of sunset' (p. 35), thus conveying a universal sense of anger. Taken altogether, we are presented with a vision of nettles, weeds and wilderness, with booming cannons and escaped convicts shackled and frozen. The nightmare scenario is made all the more terrifying in that it is viewed through the eyes of a frightened child.

The black hulk

Perhaps the most menacing image of all is the description of the prison ship to which Magwitch and Compeyson are being returned.

This simile uses a biblical reference by comparing the prison ship to Noah's ark. In the bible, God orders Noah to build an ark and rescue his family from the coming flood that will cleanse the world of the rest of sinful humanity. In Dickens' use of the image, the ark becomes a symbol of the survival of evil rather than its destruction and the clear cleansing water of God's flood has become an unclean morass of mud. Dickens again refers to 'the wicked Noah's Ark lying out on the black water' in Chapter 28 (p. 230). Once more, the water seems impure and the adjective 'black' conveys a powerful sense of evil.

Mist

The most significant symbol of the moral blindness of man occurs through the narrator's frequent references to the marshes being covered by mist. Mist also reflects the mistaken paths stumbled upon by such characters as Pip, Magwitch and Miss Havisham, all of whom are deceived by others and so 'lose their way'. In the first reference to the mist, the narrator explicitly makes a connection between physical and moral blindness.

The post showing the direction of the village is initially obscured. When Pip does locate it, the thick mist makes it appear like a ghostly finger pointing the way not so much towards the village as to the prison ships, the predominant image of evil in this early part of the novel.

Grade *booster*

Pathetic fallacy and personification are similar as personifications can also be used to give human qualities to nature.

Key quotation

...the black Hulk lying out a little way from the mud of the shore, like a wicked Noah's ark.

(Chapter 5, p. 40)

Grade *booster*

Notice the deliberate reference to Dickens' use of simile in the explanation of the Noah's ark image. Examiners love to read explanations that exhibit this level of sophistication.

Key quotation

On every rail and gate, wet lay clammy; and the marsh-mist was so thick, that the wooden finger on the post directing people to our village...was invisible to me until I was quite close under it. Then, as I looked up at it, while it dripped, it seemed to my oppressed conscience like a phantom devoting me to the Hulks.

(Chapter 3, pp. 16–17)

54

PHILIP ALLAN LITERATURE GUIDE **FOR GCSE**

This impression of a fallen world contrasts starkly with the time of year. The opening chapters take place on Christmas Eve and Christmas Day. As in Dickens' famous story *A Christmas Carol*, the timing is deliberate. It is the season when the selfless example of Christ should be foremost in people's minds, yet there is little love or compassion to be found in the young Pip's world.

London

The other great 'fallen' world depicted in the novel is that of London. Pip's first impression is that it is 'rather ugly, crooked, narrow and dirty' (Chapter 20, p. 163). Just as 'mist' pervades the marshes, dirt is a recurring motif in London. Wemmick sums up the moral calibre of both London and the age in general when he tells Pip:

> 'You may get cheated, robbed and murdered, in London. But there are plenty of people anywhere, who'll do that for you.'
>
> (Chapter 21, p. 172)

And, once again, a death image is quickly introduced:

> We entered this haven through a wicket-gate, and were disgorged by an introductory passage into a melancholy little square that looked to me like a flat burying-ground. I thought it had the most dismal trees in it, and the most dismal sparrows, and the most dismal cats, and the most dismal houses (in number half a dozen or so), that I had ever seen.
>
> (Chapter 21, p. 173)

Notice the repetition of the adjective 'dismal', another frequently used word in the novel. It suggests a general absence of vitality and life.

Victorian slums sketched by Gustave Doré.

Dickens' use of imagery

As you can see from the above analysis of Dickens' style, he is a writer who relies heavily on figurative language — that is, language which contains a high density of poetic features such as similes, metaphors, personifications and symbols. Often these images form part of an overall pattern that helps Dickens to create a particular atmosphere or to make a particular moral point. As we have already seen, Dickens uses places in this way. He also likes to reveal character through imagery. Mrs Joe, for example, is initially associated with objects that could cause pain: pins, needles, a knife, a nutmeg-grater.

Dickens does not persist in the use of this particular symbolic tag much beyond Chapter 2, but other characters are characterised by a use of imagery that follows them throughout the entire novel. Wemmick, Jaggers' clerk, is a good example of this, his associated image being that his mouth often resembles a 'post-office' (e.g. Chapter 25, p. 210). This suggests the tightening of his mouth into a narrow slit once he resumes his city persona. Another example is the extended metaphor of a castle to characterise Wemmick's house. Presumably this symbolises how his home enables him to escape his tense city personality and become the loving son of an 'aged parent'.

Whether extended or not, imagery is one of the most powerful tools Dickens uses in order to communicate with his reader and make his writing vivid (visual). Take, for example, this description of Pip's despair when he discovers that his real patron is Magwitch and not Miss Havisham after all: 'it was not until I began to think, that I began fully to know how wrecked I was, and how the ship in which I had sailed was gone to pieces'

(Chapter 39, p. 323). While you are reading through the novel, look out for imagery being used just as this metaphor has been used, simply to create a poetic picture in the reader's mind.

Grade *focus*

You are not likely to be asked a question in the exam that focuses only on style. However, in order to gain the highest grades, you will need to explain how aspects of style such as narrative tone, settings and imagery contribute to the presentation of character or theme.

Review your learning

(Answers on p. 92)

1 How would you define the term 'a writer's style'?
2 What is distinctive about Dickens' use of the narrative voice in *Great Expectations*?
3 How does Dickens make use of places in *Great Expectations*?
4 What different techniques does Dickens use in order to create humour?
5 How is Dickens' presentation of Miss Havisham, Estella and Biddy different from his presentation of Mrs Joe and why do you think this might be?
6 Why does Dickens not use cartoon violence in his presentation of Orlick?

More interactive questions and answers online.

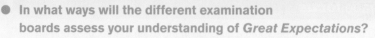

Tackling the assessments

- In what ways will the different examination boards assess your understanding of *Great Expectations*?
- How should you plan and structure examination essays?
- How should you respond to other types of assessment tasks?
- How should you provide evidence to support your interpretation of the text?
- How should you analyse metaphors, similes and personifications?
- What will turn a grade-C essay into a grade-A* essay?

Higher and foundation tiers

You will be entered for the GCSE English Literature examination at either foundation or higher tier. The foundation tier allows you a grade between C and G. The foundation-tier questions are easier than those for the higher tier. The higher tier allows you to get a grade between A* and D. However, if you don't score enough marks for a D grade, you may well be unclassified. Your teacher decides which tier to enter you for, based on your work during the course.

Examination boards and types of assessment

Of the various examination boards, only AQA and Edexcel are currently setting *Great Expectations* as a set text for GCSE English Literature. Exactly how you will be assessed will depend on which examination board you are following. The table on p. 59 indicates which parts of the AQA and Edexcel GCSE English Literature and GCSE English Language qualifications allow you to answer on *Great Expectations*. It also shows the percentage of the total GCSE marks that each form of assessment assigns to *Great Expectations*.

	AQA GCSE English Lit	AQA GCSE English Lang	Edexcel GCSE English Lit	Edexcel GCSE English Lang
Exam	Yes	No	Yes	No
Percentage of total GCSE marks	15%	—	25%	—
Controlled Assessment	Yes	Yes	No	No
Percentage of total GCSE marks	25% (but also includes a response to a Shakespeare play)	15%	—	—

How will you be assessed by AQA?

In the AQA English Literature GCSE, *Great Expectations* falls under two different possible modes of assessment. One assessment mode is via an externally set and assessed examination called **Unit 4: Approaching Shakespeare and the English Literary Heritage**. This consists of:

- a **Shakespeare** question worth 20% of the total GCSE marks, for which you will be allowed 50 minutes
- a **Prose from the English Literary Heritage** question worth 15% of the total GCSE marks, for which you will be allowed 40 minutes. *Great Expectations* is one of the set texts for this section

You are expected to take into the examination an unannotated (clean) copy of both *Great Expectations* and the Shakespeare play that you have been studying.

Alternatively, AQA allows for the assessment of *Great Expectations* via a Controlled Assessment Task called **Unit 3: The Significance of Shakespeare and the English Literary Heritage**. If your under- standing of *Great Expectations* is to be examined as a Controlled Assessment Task, the overall marks for this unit will constitute 25% of your total GCSE mark. In this task you will write about *Great Expectations* and a Shakespeare play that you have studied during the GCSE course. The type of assessment that you eventually take will be decided by your English teacher.

As you are most likely being entered for English Language as well as English Literature, you may also be studying *Great Expectations* for the reading Controlled Assessment Task in English Language: **AQA GCSE English Language Unit 3: Understanding spoken and written texts and writing creatively – Part a: Extended reading**. This is worth 15% of the total GCSE marks and the recommended number of words is 1,200.

How will you be assessed by Edexcel?

For Edexcel, *Great Expectations* falls under one form of assessment only called **Unit 1: Understanding Prose**. This is an externally set and assessed examination paper which requires you to answer a question on one **Different Cultures and Traditions** prose text and a question on one **Literary Heritage** prose text. *Great Expectations* is one of the set texts for the **Literary Heritage** prose text section of this exam. You will be allowed 1 hour and 45 minutes to complete both questions.

This examination paper is worth 50% of the total GCSE marks but the percentage is equally divided between your responses to both sections of the paper. Therefore, your response to the *Great Expectations* question will be worth 25% of the total GCSE marks. You are expected to take an unannotated copy of *Great Expectations* and of your **Different Cultures and Traditions** prose text into the examination with you.

There is no option to respond to *Great Expectations* as part of a Controlled Assessment Task. Similarly, it is not possible to answer on *Great Expectations* for Edexcel English Language.

Approaching the questions

How do you refer to the author?

You can refer to Dickens either by name or as 'the author'. You should avoid using his first name, Charles, as this suggests that you know him personally and thus makes your writing sound immature. As his name ends in an 's' you can refer to 'Dickens' use of…' as opposed to 'Dickens's use of…', which sounds a little clumsy.

What is the most appropriate writing style?

As this is a formal assessment, you should write in a formal style. Examiners' reports every year give examples of inappropriate language used by candidates. Don't make the same mistake. This means:

- **Do not** use colloquial language or slang (except when quoting dialogue from the actual text): 'Pip becomes a right jerk once he gets his dosh'.
- **Do not** become too personal: 'I wouldn't mind going out with that Estella bird if she wasn't so stuck up!'
- **Do** use suitable phrases for an academic essay: for example, 'It could be argued that…' rather than 'I reckon that…'.

Should you refer to yourself?

At one time it was thought to be a bad thing to write in the first person (using 'I') in GCSE work. This is now acceptable but the frequency with which you refer to yourself depends on the phrasing of the question. Look carefully at the wording of the AQA foundation- and higher-tier examination questions on pp. 62 and 63 of this guide. You will see that the foundation-tier question directly addresses *you* and invites a personal response. The higher-tier question refers to *the reader* and so requires a much more impersonal response in which you should refer to the impact of the novel on the reader rather than on yourself.

Why should you plan an essay?

If you are feeling under pressure in the exam, it is tempting to read questions quickly and to start writing immediately as in a timed situation every minute counts. However, this can be a grave error! You should read the question carefully, at least twice, and attempt to break it down into parts to work out exactly what you are being asked to do. This will help to ensure that you answer the question that is being asked and not the one that you think is being asked — or the one that you hope is being asked. It will also help to ensure that you don't run out of ideas halfway through your answer.

Before you begin to plan, underline key words in the question. You should practise underlining or highlighting the key words in every new question you meet.

Why should you check your answer?

If you have any time left, it is a good idea to read through your answer to check for spelling, punctuation and grammar (SPAG) errors. It is clearly stated in both the AQA and Edexcel specifications that the quality of your written communication will be assessed. If your SPAG is inaccurate, this could prevent you from gaining the grade that you would otherwise have deserved.

Tackling the AQA exam essay

The AQA GCSE English Literature examination requires you to write an essay. This is true for both foundation and higher students. A good essay follows a clear structure:

- an introduction, in which you demonstrate your understanding of the question and in which you might indicate key ideas that you intend to investigate

- the main body of the essay, where your ideas are presented in a logical sequence of points supported by the essential components of evidence and explanation (PEE)
- a conclusion, in which you sum up the main points that you have made in your essay

Whatever you are asked to write about, your first challenge is to read the question carefully and then plan your essay.

> ### Pause for thought ⏸
>
> If you have ever watched a news bulletin, you may have noticed a similar structure in action. In the opening minute, the main news items are announced. Then each of these items is explored in detail, with evidence provided to prove that they are true and accurate. In the last few minutes, there is a summary reminding the viewer of what has been said.

Foundation tier

Here is an example of an AQA GCSE English Literature foundation-tier examination question:

> You are advised to spend about 40 minutes on this question.
>
> Answer both parts a) and b).
>
> a) What are your feelings for Pip before and after he receives his 'great expectations'? Remember to write about the society in which Pip lives. **(12 marks)**
>
> b) How does Dickens show you what Pip's character is like in these two different parts of the novel? **(12 marks)**

> ### Grade *booster* ❗
>
> To ensure that you answer the question correctly, spend five minutes breaking the question up into a list of its various parts.

In effect, this question is providing you with the following four-point plan:

- What do you feel about Pip before Jaggers informs him that he is to become a gentleman?
- How do you feel about Pip after he has been given the news that he is to become a gentleman?
- What do you learn about Pip's society?
- How does Dickens show you what Pip's character is like in these two different parts of the novel?

> ### Grade *booster* ❗
>
> When responding to a multi-part question, keep a close eye on how many marks are allocated for each separate part. A good candidate is always aware of how much time to spend on each question — or each part of a question.

Higher tier

Here is an example of an AQA GCSE English Literature higher-tier examination question:

> You are advised to spend about 40 minutes on this question.
>
> How does Dickens encourage the reader to feel differently about Pip in different parts of the novel? Remember to write about the society in which Pip lives. **(24 marks)**

Grade *booster*

Examiners' reports stress that in an 'open' question like this, there is a danger of trying to cover too much ground. Therefore, in your introduction, you could explain that your focus will be mainly on two significant incidents. This will then allow you to probe Dickens' methods of influencing the reader's emotions in depth.

If you were answering the higher-tier question, you would have to spend five minutes making a plan for yourself. It might look something like this, though it is unlikely to be as detailed owing to the time constraints you will be working under:

● Explain what Pip is like during one episode before he becomes a gentleman, especially his attitude towards Joe.

● Explain how Dickens reveals Pip's nature in this part of the novel — that is, how Dickens establishes Pip's character through his behaviour, speech, thoughts and feelings and through the tone of the narrative voice which reveals how the older Pip feels about his younger self.

● Explain how these techniques encourage the reader to feel sympathetic towards Pip at this point in the novel.

● Using an episode from later in the novel, explain how once Pip becomes a gentleman he suddenly becomes aloof, snobbish and unaffectionate towards those who had previously showed him nothing but kindness.

● Explain how Dickens uses the same techniques as above in order to reveal these new aspects of Pip's character.

● Explain how these techniques encourage the reader to disapprove of Pip's behaviour at this point in the novel.

● Through the transformation which takes place in Pip's personality between these two different parts of the novel, explain what impression Dickens is creating about the society in which Pip lives.

Similarities and differences

As you can see, both of the above AQA questions are asking you to write about the following things:

- the personality of the main character and how it changes during the course of the novel
- how the reader feels about Pip at different stages of the novel
- what Pip's progress reveals about the society in which he lives
- most importantly, what techniques Dickens uses to reveal the various changes in Pip's character to the reader

A subtle difference is that the higher-tier question requires you to write about the impact of Dickens' characterisation on *the reader* rather than on *you* personally. A more obvious difference is that the foundation-tier question is broken into two sections, thus making the task a little easier as it contains more guidance and essentially provides you with an essay plan.

Tackling the Edexcel exam question

In the Edexcel GCSE English Literature examination you are given an extract to read followed by a question divided into four parts. In the examples below, page references are given rather than the complete extract.

Foundation tier

The approximate amount of time to spend on this question is 50 minutes.

Read the extract from *Great Expectations* which is taken from Chapter 27, p. 222. It begins 'I really believe Joe would have prolonged this word...' and ends '...I was conscious of a sort of dignity in the look'.

Answer all parts of the question that follows as fully as possible.

a) Outline the key events that lead up to this extract from the beginning of Volume II. (10)

b) Explain how the writer presents the relationship between Pip and Joe in this extract. Use evidence from the extract to support your answer. **(10)**

c) From this extract, what do you learn about the character of Joe? Use evidence from the extract to support your answer. **(8)**

d) Explain Pip's attitude to Joe in one other part of the novel. Use examples of the writer's language to support your answer. **(12)**

(Total: 40 marks)

Higher tier

Again, the approximate amount of time to spend on this question is 50 minutes. Use the same extract from Chapter 27 (see above) in order to answer the question.

Answer all parts of the question as fully as possible.

a) Explain how the writer presents the character of Joe in this extract. Use evidence from the extract to support your answer. **(8)**

b) Comment on the effect of the language used to show the relationship between Pip and Joe in the extract. Use evidence from the extract to support your answer. **(10)**

c) Explore the importance of social class in this extract. Use evidence from the extract to support your answer. **(10)**

d) Explore the importance of social class in one other part of the novel. Use examples of the writer's language to support your answer. **(12)**

(Total: 40 marks)

Similarities and differences

If you look carefully at both sets of questions, you will see that there are a number of similarities. Both tiers:

- test your understanding of Pip and Joe and of the nature of the relationship between them
- require you to explore another section of the novel that is in some way related to this extract
- require you to use the essential analytical tool of PEE (point, evidence, explanation)

The main difference is that whereas the foundation-tier paper mainly asks you to respond to questions concerning plot and character, the higher-tier paper has a much greater emphasis on Dickens' use of language and also directly addresses the issue of theme.

Grade *booster*

Whichever examination board you are following, you will need to have a good understanding of: the plot, the main themes, the main characters and how they relate to these themes, the narrative viewpoint and Dickens' use of language.

Tackling the AQA Controlled Assessment

The full title of this Controlled Assessment Task is **AQA GCSE English Literature Unit 3: The Significance of Shakespeare and the English Literary Heritage**. If you are taking this assessment, it is because your teacher has decided that you should be examined on *Great Expectations* and your Shakespeare text in this way rather than by examination. This assessment is completed in school, probably in class, and will most likely be supervised by your English teacher. Controlled Assessment Tasks have replaced the coursework element of the old GCSEs and cannot be completed at home or unsupervised. The Controlled Assessment Task must be undertaken under examination conditions, so your teacher cannot help you and you are not allowed to communicate with other students. However, as this is a reading assessment, you will be allowed to use a dictionary, a thesaurus and a grammar and spellcheck program, if you are using a computer.

You are allowed to prepare for the task in advance with your teacher and you can take brief notes into the assessment, but you are not allowed to take in detailed notes or a planning grid. Your notes must also be in your own words. You are allowed up to four hours to complete this task and the length of your response should be about 2,000 words.

Although you will be writing about a Shakespeare play as well as *Great Expectations* and will be exploring a common link, you are not required to write *in detail* about similarities or differences between the texts. However, you are expected to draw links in your introduction and conclusion. Some candidates may wish to make more explicit links throughout (AO3). However, you are required to refer to the social, historical and cultural context of the two different texts (AO4).

This unit is worth 25% of the total GCSE marks. The objectives assessed in this unit are as follows:

- **AO1** — respond to texts critically and imaginatively; select and evaluate relevant textual detail to illustrate and support interpretations.

- **AO2** — explain how language, structure and form contribute to writers' presentation of ideas, themes and settings.
- **AO3** — explain links between texts, evaluating writers' different ways of expressing meaning and achieving effects.
- **AO4** — relate texts to their social, cultural and historical contexts; explain how texts have been influential and significant to self and other readers in different contexts and at different times.

The relative values of these four Assessment Objectives in relation to this unit are indicated in the table below:

Assessment Objective	Percentage of total GCSE marks
AO1	5%
AO2	10%
AO3	5%
AO4	5%
Total	**25%**

The tasks are divided into two categories but you only choose one task. Below is an example of what an AQA GCSE English Literature Controlled Assessment Task looks like:

Themes and ideas	Characterisation and voice
Explore the ways writers explore manipulation in the texts you have studied.	Explore the ways writers present the central character in the two texts you have studied.
Explore the ways writers explore friendship in the texts you have studied.	Explore the ways writers present romantic relationships in the two texts that you have studied.

Your teacher will then be able to contextualise these tasks into something more meaningful for you — but, remember, you only have to write on one task. For example, the first of the 'Themes and ideas' tasks could be contextualised as follows:

Explore the consequences of manipulation in *Macbeth* and *Great Expectations*.

In order to answer this question, you would need to develop a plan that takes into account the relative values of the four Assessment Objectives outlined above. For more on the Assessment Objectives, see *Assessment Objectives and skills* starting on p. 74.

The vital importance of using PEE

One of the essential tools of literary criticism is the use of PEE (point, evidence, explanation). In fact, this is the technique that has been used in order to write this guide!

For the AQA examination, a brief plan is suggested by the foundation-tier examination paper and this contains the key points that the examiner wants you to develop. However, for the higher tier, you have to devise your own plan with your own set of points that will answer the question effectively. For the Edexcel examination, the planning has largely been done for you, as the points are actually provided in the form of the four-part question. However, whichever form of examination paper you take, the key thing is to develop your points through an effective use of PEE.

Point

It stands to reason that every section of your essay should begin with a point which directly relates to the essay title. The better thought out these points are, the better your essay will be.

Evidence

Pause for thought

Think about the evidence part of PEE as giving evidence in court. Imagine yourself as the prosecution counsel providing evidence to support your accusation. With his interest in the theme of justice, Dickens would have approved!

Every point must be supported by evidence in the form of either:
- a quotation

or

- a reference to a part of the novel in which you use your own words to describe the evidence

This second form of evidence involves the use of paraphrasing and is especially useful if you need to sum up a lengthy passage.

The purpose of evidence is to prove to the examiner that you have a good knowledge of the text and that your point is accurate. You can use paraphrasing when dealing with such aspects of *Great Expectations* as structure, theme, characterisation and context. However, you must use quotation when analysing the tone of the narrative voice or other aspects of Dickens' use of language. Both AQA and Edexcel allow you to take the text into the exam or Controlled Assessment Task (remember, though, that it must not be annotated) so finding the quotations is a matter of knowing the text well.

Using quotations effectively comes down to five principles:

1 Making the context of the quotation clear — that is, briefly explaining how the section of the text where the quotation appears relates to the rest of the text.

2 Putting inverted commas at the beginning and end of the quoted words.

3 Writing the quotation exactly as it appears in the text.

4 Keeping quotations as short as possible.

5 Not repeating the exact words of the quotation in your explanation of it as this will not show the examiner that you have understood it.

Grade *booster*

There is no need to tell the examiner that you are using a quotation as there are quotation marks to make this clear. Begin your explanation with a phrase such as: 'This makes it sound as if…/creates the impression…/makes the reader feel…/conveys a sense of…'.

Separate quotations

The first kind of quotation you can use is the separate quotation and this is particularly appropriate for longer quotations. This is where you make your point, then give the evidence as a quotation on a separate line, followed by your explanation of why this quotation is significant to the point that you are making:

When Pip first appears in Chapter 1, it is clear that Dickens immediately intends to create sympathy for him:

'the small bundle of shivers growing afraid of it all and beginning to cry, was Pip'.

The use of such emotive words as 'small', 'shivers', 'afraid' and 'cry' suggests the vulnerability of the child all alone in the graveyard and so encourages the reader to feel concerned about his wellbeing.

Embedded quotations

An embedded quotation is one that runs on from your own words on the same line and is more appropriate for shorter quotations:

The narrator's description of how the young Pip 'pleaded in terror' for his life when Magwitch suddenly pounces on him further heightens the reader's sense of alarm.

This kind of quotation works best if the sentence as a whole, with the quotation, is grammatically correct. You can use brackets [...] to alter the verb tense or to replace a pronoun with a noun to make your quotation flow with your own sentence.

Using ellipsis

If the quotation that you wish to use as evidence is too long, you can shorten it by using an ellipsis ... .

'As I never saw my father or my mother...my first fancies regarding what they were like, were unreasonably derived from their tombstones.'

Referring to the text by use of paraphrase

You could have provided the above piece of evidence by simply referring to the text in your own words:

Another way in which Dickens creates sympathy for Pip is by immediately establishing him as an orphan on the opening page of the text when Pip is visiting the graves of his deceased parents.

Explanation

The final part of the winning PEE formula is the explanation. The more sophisticated your explanation, the better your answer is likely to be. Look back at the various pieces of evidence given above. They are all accompanied by explanations that tell the examiner how the evidence proves the point that the student is making. In these examples, the student is showing that when Pip first appears in the novel, it is clear that Dickens intends to create sympathy for him. However, you would only be credited for developing this point *if it was relevant to the essay title*. The above, for example, would be effective as part of an answer to either of the following questions:

How does Dickens make the reader feel about Pip before and after he is told of his 'great expectations'?

Or

Referring to two different characters within the novel, show how Dickens presents childhood.

How to analyse imagery

Similes, metaphors and personification can be referred to as figures of speech or imagery. Writers use these techniques in order to create a more vivid (visual) impression of what they are trying to describe, or in order to create a particular atmosphere/tone which could, for example, be romantic, tragic, dramatic or humorous.

Simile

A simile is a comparison in which one thing is said to be like or as another thing: '...the chamberlain had brought me in...an object like the ghost of a walking-cane...'.

Metaphor

A metaphor is a comparison in which one thing is said to be something else which it literally is not *or* when something is said to be able to do something which it literally cannot do: '...with a despotic monster of a four-post bedstead...'.

Personification

Personification is a technique by which an inanimate (non-living) thing — **or** other non-human thing **or** abstract quality/idea — is given human qualities which it literally cannot possess: 'When I had lain awake a little while, those extraordinary voices with which silence teems, began to make themselves audible. The closet whispered, the fireplace sighed ...'.

The five-part formula

All the above images come from Chapter 45, in which Pip describes a most uncomfortable night spent at the Hummums Hotel, shortly after he has learned that Estella is to marry Drummle and immediately after he has been given a mysterious note warning him not to go home. The purpose of the five-part formula that follows is to help you when you are using PEE. If you are finding it difficult to explain why or how a writer has used a simile, metaphor or personification, then you could use this simple process:

1 Copy out the figure of speech in quotation marks.
2 State which figure of speech it is.
3 Say what the original thing being described is.
4 Say what it is said to be like/as (SIMILE), or what it is said to be/be able to do (METAPHOR), or what human qualities it is said to possess (PERSONIFICATION).
5 Find as many impressions as possible that have been created about the original thing by use of the figure of speech.
  By doing this you will, in effect, have used PEE.

Example

1 '…with a despotic monster of a four-post bedstead in it, straddling over the whole place, putting one of his arbitrary legs into the fireplace and another into the doorway, and squeezing the wretched little washing-stand in quite a Divinely Righteous manner'
2 In this metaphor,
3 the original thing being described is the four-post bed.
4 The author is comparing it to a monster.
5 The impressions created by this comparison are that: the bed is far too big for the room, the room itself is uncomfortable and cramped, and the room is somehow threatening to Pip. Dickens is using this nightmarish image, along with the other frightening images of the ghost simile and the 'extraordinary voices' personifications, in order to suggest how startled Pip is about the warning note from Wemmick as well as how distressed he is feeling after the meeting with Estella and Miss Havisham in which Estella revealed that she is to marry Drummle.

Text focus

Read the extract in Chapter 45, pp. 366–67 which begins 'Turning from the Temple gate…' and ends 'in every one of those staring rounds I saw written, DON'T GO HOME'. Make a note of how many different images Dickens uses in order to create an impression of Pip's anxiety.

Grade *focus*

C-grade answers frequently consist of a series of PEE points where explanations of evidence fail to probe deeply. Such explanations may do little more than simply repeat what the quotation says but in the student's own words. To reach the higher grades, you should also try to analyse more sophisticated aspects of the evidence such as features of style. You might, for example, explain how the use of language has been deliberately designed to deepen the emotional impact of the situation on the reader or to make the writing more vivid (visual). This will help you to reach the A or A* grades.

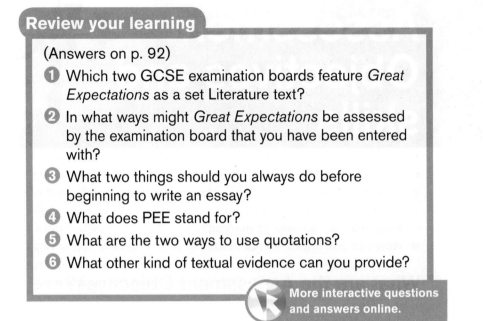

Review your learning

(Answers on p. 92)

1 Which two GCSE examination boards feature *Great Expectations* as a set Literature text?

2 In what ways might *Great Expectations* be assessed by the examination board that you have been entered with?

3 What two things should you always do before beginning to write an essay?

4 What does PEE stand for?

5 What are the two ways to use quotations?

6 What other kind of textual evidence can you provide?

More interactive questions and answers online.

Assessment Objectives and skills

- What are the Assessment Objectives?
- How do the Assessment Objectives apply to AQA and Edexcel?
- How will your answer be marked?
- How can you improve your grade?

What are the Assessment Objectives?

The Assessment Objectives that you will be marked on are:

- **AO1** — respond to texts critically and imaginatively; select and evaluate relevant textual detail to illustrate and support interpretations.
- **AO2** — explain how language, structure and form contribute to writers' presentation of ideas, themes and settings.
- **AO3** — explain links between texts, evaluating writers' different ways of expressing meaning and achieving effects.
- **AO4** — relate texts to their social, cultural and historical contexts; explain how texts have been influential and significant to self and other readers in different contexts and at different times.

Applying the AOs to AQA and Edexcel

AQA

If you are being entered for AQA GCSE English Literature, you will be assessed on *Great Expectations* either by the Unit 3 Controlled Assessment Task, or by the Unit 4 examination. For more on this, see p. 59 in *Tackling the assessments*. The table on p. 75 tells you the percentage of total GCSE marks that the four Assessment Objectives are worth in relation to these AQA units.

Unit	Form of assessment	AO1	AO2	AO3	AO4	Percentage of total GCSE marks
3	Controlled Assessment Task	5%	10%	5%	5%	25%
4	Examination	15%	15%	0%	5%	35%

As you can see, AO3 is not assessed in the Unit 4 examination. In addition, the Unit 4 examination is worth more marks than the Controlled Assessment Task.

Edexcel

For Edexcel GCSE English Literature, *Great Expectations* is assessed by examination only. The table below tells you the percentage of total GCSE marks that the four Assessment Objectives are worth in relation to the Edexcel examination.

Unit	Form of assessment	AO1	AO2	AO3	AO4	Percentage of total GCSE marks
1	Examination	25%	10%	0%	15%	50%

How is your answer marked?

An examiner can only give you marks in relation to how well your answer fulfils the relevant Assessment Objectives for the task.

AO1

'Respond to texts critically and imaginatively; select and evaluate relevant textual detail to illustrate and support interpretations.'

- **'Respond to texts critically...'**: you must say what you think of *Great Expectations* and why. You must show that you can evaluate the novel and understand that in writing it, Dickens has had to make numerous decisions, such as the big decisions about plot, characterisation and settings. You should also express your opinion about how successful these decisions have been.
- **'...and imaginatively'**: you are expected to show a creative, original response to the text. You must use your own imagination in order to consider why Dickens has made the various decisions that he has made. For example, why has Dickens decided that Miss Havisham

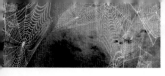

should be so full of hate? This Assessment Objective also requires you to understand that there is no single way to interpret a work of literature. Interpretation is determined by your own experiences of life. A middle-aged woman who has recently been deserted by her husband will most likely have a far greater understanding of Miss Havisham than a teenage boy who might simply dismiss Miss Havisham's behaviour as ridiculous.

Grade *booster*

There is a big difference between the reason why Miss Havisham is so full of hate and the reason why Dickens has decided to make her so full of hate. Remember, characters are not real people and writers choose to create them in particular ways for particular purposes.

Pause for thought

Once a work of literature is published, people will immediately begin to interpret it in their own way, often seeing things that the writer had not necessarily intended. Does this mean that because the writer had not intended it, the reader's interpretation is wrong?

Grade *booster*

PEE yet again! Point, evidence, explanation.

- **'select…relevant textual detail to illustrate and support interpretations'**: you should support your views by providing evidence in the form of short quotations from the text or by referring to details in the text in your own words.
- **'…evaluate…'**: you should explain to the examiner how the evidence that you have provided proves that your interpretation of a particular aspect of the novel is valid.

AO2

'Explain how language, structure and form contribute to writers' presentation of ideas, themes and settings.'

- **'language, structure and form…'**: the word 'language' refers to Dickens' choice of words. Look at the first description of Pip in the novel. Dickens deliberately uses a number of words which create sympathy for Pip by emphasising his vulnerability: '…that small bundle of shivers growing afraid of it all and beginning to cry, was Pip' (Chapter 1, p. 4). 'Structure' refers to the overall shape of the novel as discussed in the *Plot and structure* section of this guide. Remember that the novel is divided into three volumes which each relate a different phase of Pip's life. 'Form' means that you are being asked to consider how Dickens' decision to write his story as a novel — rather than, say, as a play or narrative poem — affects the way he presents ideas, themes or settings. For example, if he had written *Great Expectations* as a play, it would have been far more difficult to make as much use of settings as he has done in the novel. However, he would have been able to develop many of the same themes.

● **'ideas, themes and settings...'**: the difference between ideas and themes is subtle. A theme is an idea that is given major prominence in the novel, such as the theme of social class, whereas an idea might be introduced but not fully developed. Themes and settings are covered in great detail in the *Themes* and *Style* sections of this guide.

● This Assessment Objective is basically asking you to reflect on how the building blocks of the novel (language, structure and form) determine some of the contents of the novel (ideas, themes and settings).

AO3

'Explain links between texts, evaluating writers' different ways of expressing meaning and achieving effects.'

● **'links between texts...'**: for your study of *Great Expectations*, this Assessment Objective is only relevant to the AQA Controlled Assessment Task **Unit 3: The significance of Shakespeare and the English Literary Heritage**. If you are being assessed in this way, you are only expected to explain the links between the Shakespeare play and *Great Expectations* in the introduction and conclusion to your 2,000 word response. The link that you will be exploring will be either a common theme or an aspect of characterisation: for example, the similarities and differences between the ways in which Shakespeare and Dickens explore the theme of evil in *Macbeth* and *Great Expectations.*

● **'evaluating writers' different ways of expressing meaning and achieving effects...'**: you are being asked to appraise the two texts and explain how both writers make an impact on the reader (Dickens) or the audience (Shakespeare). This will involve you writing about *Great Expectations* as a novel to be read and the Shakespeare text as a play to be watched. This is an important distinction. You will be making judgements about such areas as how the authors encourage the reader *or* the audience *or* you to feel about the main character(s) and what techniques they use to create these feelings. Or you will be making judgements about how the two writers present a similar theme and, again, the ways in which their handling of this theme will have an effect on the reader/audience/you.

AO4

'Relate texts to their social, cultural and historical contexts; explain how texts have been influential and significant to self and other readers in different contexts and at different times.'

If you are trying to display knowledge of this area, do not treat the English Literature exam or Controlled Assessment Task as though it were a history test. Your task is to write about the text and so any background historical information you provide should be relevant to the exam question, closely related to the text, and included only to demonstrate your understanding about the aspect of the text that you are writing about. For example, some reference to the great inequalities which existed between the classes in Dickensian England is obviously relevant to an essay question which asks you to consider how becoming a gentleman changes Pip's attitudes and behaviour.

- **'relate texts to their social, cultural and historical contexts...'**: this is of importance when you are studying a literary heritage text such as *Great Expectations* because the text was written in mid-Victorian England when people lived in a different society from ours and lived by a different set of values. If Dickens were alive today, he would undoubtedly write a different novel, as he would be influenced by other life experiences and would have been exposed to a different set of ideas. See the *Context* section of this guide for more information on the ways in which Dickens' writing was influenced by the times in which he lived.

- **'explain how texts have been influential and significant to self and other readers in different contexts and at different times...'**: this objective certainly encourages you to write about how you personally have been affected through your exposure to the text. However, it also asks you to acknowledge that other readers may react differently to the text if they are from a different time period or if they live in a different country or if they are from a different social or ethnic background within the same country. Therefore, you might consider how a modern reader would view *Great Expectations* differently from one of Dickens' contemporaries. For example, a modern reader living in the UK might well be shocked by the number of execution sentences which the judge passes at the end of Magwitch's trial in Chapter 56, 'two-and-thirty men and women' (p. 457), because we live in a society which has long since dispensed with capital punishment.

What you will not get marks for

The Assessment Objectives tell you what you *will* get marks for. It is also important to know what you *will not* get marks for.

Retelling the story

You can be certain that the examiner marking your essay already knows the plot of *Great Expectations* and does not want to be told the story again. The examiner follows a mark scheme and will probably be referring to 'grade descriptors' — these outline the features to be expected from essays at each of the grades. A key feature of the lowest grades, as identified by the grade descriptors, is 'retelling the story' — so do not do it!

Quoting long passages

You will waste time and gain no marks by quoting long passages from the novel. As you are allowed to take your copy of *Great Expectations* into the exam or Controlled Assessment Task (AQA), there is a temptation for those who have not prepared thoroughly to make answers longer by copying out chunks of the text — or to copy out chunks of the extract given for extract-based questions (Edexcel). It wastes time and doesn't get marks, so don't do it! Use your judgement: it is rarely necessary to quote more than two sentences at a time.

Identifying figures of speech or other features

You will not gain marks simply for identifying images such as similes or metaphors. Similarly, you will gain no marks for pointing out that 'Dickens uses a lot of adjectives in this passage'. You will gain marks only by identifying these features and then continuing to say why the author has used them and how effective you think they are.

Giving unsubstantiated opinions

The examiner will be keen to give you marks for your opinions but only if they are supported by reasoned argument and references to the text. Therefore, you will get no marks for writing 'Everyone thinks that Joe is completely stupid but I don't'. You will get marks for:

It is easy to dismiss Joe as being illiterate and unintelligent but it is important to remember that Joe's father was an alcoholic and, as Joe explains to Pip in Chapter 7, disrupted every chance of schooling that his mother tried to give him. Despite this great disadvantage, he has been able to master a complex trade and, when the opportunity for education does come to him in the form of Biddy, he does learn to read and write. Furthermore, Joe has a natural morality and an innate wisdom which means that he is frequently able to give the young Pip sound advice. A good example of this occurs in Chapter 9 when Joe warns Pip against dishonesty: 'If you can't get to be oncommon through going straight, you'll never get to do it through going crooked.'

This candidate opens by immediately making clear what point is being made. This point presents a reasoned and insightful interpretation of Joe and also shows an awareness of other possible viewpoints. The point is then backed up by evidence from the text. Finally, the candidate explains how each piece of evidence used supports the sophisticated interpretation of Joe's character.

Grade *focus*

Knowing what the examiner is looking for is essential. To gain an A*, you would need to fulfil all of the grade-A requirements plus include what examiners describe as the additional quality of 'flair'. This means that little something extra that makes your answer stand out from the crowd. It could, for example, be the originality of your interpretation coupled with a rigorous use of evidence to support your point of view.

Grade	Description
A	Candidates respond enthusiastically and critically to texts, showing imagination and originality in developing alternative approaches and interpretations.
	They confidently explore and evaluate how language, structure and form contribute to writers' varied ways of presenting ideas, themes and settings, and how they achieve specific effects on readers.
	Candidates make illuminating connections and comparisons between texts.
	They identify and comment on the impact of the social, cultural and historical contexts of texts on different readers at different times.
	They convey ideas persuasively and cogently, supporting them with apt textual references.
C	Candidates understand and demonstrate how writers use ideas, themes and settings in texts to affect the reader.
	They respond personally to the effects of language, structure and form, referring to textual detail to support their views and reactions.
	They explain the relevance and impact of connections and comparisons between texts.
	They show awareness of some of the social, cultural and historical contexts of texts and of how this influences their meanings for contemporary and modern readers.
	They convey ideas clearly and appropriately.

Review your learning

(Answers on p. 92)

1. Which is the only GCSE English Literature Unit which assesses AO3?

2. How will your answer be marked?

3. Why should you write about characters as creations of the writer rather than as real people?

4. Name four things identified in this section that would waste your time and gain you no extra marks in the exam.

5. Why is it important to substantiate your interpretation of the text with evidence?

6. What factors might encourage another reader to interpret the text in a different way from you?

More interactive questions and answers online.

Sample essays

- What are the features of grade-C and grade-A* answers?
- What are examiners looking for when they assess your work?
- What do a good introduction and conclusion look like?
- What does effective use of PEE look like?

Four sample answers are provided below — two answers at grade C and two answers at grade A*. The answers are responses to two different types of question: a character-based question and a theme-based question, one question from each relevant exam board. It is suggested that you read the grade-C answers first and see how you could improve on them. Then read the A* answers. Remember that there are often many different good approaches to the same essay.

Whichever examination board you have been entered for, it is worthwhile reading both sets of answers. Both show you what examiners are looking for and, therefore, how you can improve your grade. They will also add to your knowledge and understanding of *Great Expectations*.

For guidance regarding aspects of successful essay writing, such as planning, using quotation and using the essential analytical tool of PEE (point, evidence, explanation), see the *Tackling the assessments* section of this guide.

AQA

Higher-tier character-based question

You are advised to spend about 40 minutes on this question.

Great Expectations is a tale of personal growth. Referring to two different characters in the novel, look at the various ways in which Dickens presents characters who grow and those who stay the same.

Remember to write about the society they live in.

Grade-C answer

Dickens has lots of characters in his book. Some of them change and some of them stay the same. In this essay I am going to look at two different characters Pip and Compeyson. Pip changes a lot during the novel but Compeyson is evil from start to finish.**1**

At the start of the book, Pip is a just a child. We see him in a graveyard when an escaped convict jumps out and surprises him: 'Hold your noise…or I'll cut your throat!'**2** This makes the reader feel sorry for Pip as he must be frightened out of his mind.**3** Magwitch tells Pip that he must steal food and a file from Joe. This immediately creates suspense as Pip is torn between his love for Joe and his fear of the convict.**4** Also, because he is honest, he does not want to break his word to Magwitch.

'I was afraid to sleep, even if I had been inclined, for I knew that at the first faint dawn of morning I must rob the pantry.' (Chapter 2)

Pip cannot sleep because of the guilt that he is feeling and this shows how honest he really is. Also, he does not want to rob**5** from Joe because he loves him so much. In Chapter 6 he says:

'I do not recall that i felt any tenderness of conscience in reference to Mrs Joe, when the fear of being found out was lifted off me. But I loved Joe…'**6**

Later on in the book after he becomes a gentleman there is a big change in Pip's personality and he no longer shows as much love for Joe. This is because he loves Estella more and feels that she would not like him having close friends like Joe. When Joe comes to visit him in London in Chapter 27, Pip makes Joe feel so awkward that he keeps dropping his hat and starts to call Pip 'Sir'.**7** This is because Pip is now a gentleman and so Joe is unsure how to behave around him.**8**

By the end of the novel, Pip is a changed man. He has grown up a lot because he has realised that he is not meant to be with Estella after all and so there is no longer any point being a snob towards Joe and Biddy. He also comes to love Magwitch as if he was his father and cares for him after he gets injured by the steamer. He also tries to save Magwitch's life by trying to get him an appeal. In fact he tries so hard, he makes himself ill. This shows that Pip has become more mature because when Magwitch first told Pip that he was his benefactor Pip was disgusted and did not want Magwitch to touch him. But now it is Pip who is touching Magwitch as he holds Magwitch's hand when he is dying. I think that this would make the reader really respect Pip and think that he is a more moral person now. Dickens has shown that Pip is a much better man when he is no longer a gentleman than when he was a gentleman and this is the point of the book.**9**

1 Not a subtle introduction but it does make clear what the candidate intends to do and it does relevantly address the essay question.

2 Good use of ellipsis to shorten the quotation.

3 Reasonably effective explanation. Clear evidence of PEE being used here.

4 Good use of textual reference which is accompanied by a pleasing explanation of the effect on the reader.

5 Weak vocabulary which suggests a lack of sophistication with this candidate.

6 Reasonably effective use of PEE again, although the quotation has not been copied accurately — small 'i'.

7 Shows a good understanding of Pip's motivation here and of the fact that Pip is making Joe more awkward than he would normally be.

8 A pleasing recognition of the historical context.

9 An effective paragraph that shows a reasonably sophisticated understanding of why Pip changes again towards the end of the novel. Some good evidence is provided to support the candidate's interpretation. Also demonstrates a good understanding of how Dickens is using Pip to develop a major theme.

10 Again, displays a pleasing awareness that Dickens is using character to develop theme. Unfortunately, initially misspells Compeyson's name.

11 Another example of the unsophisticated vocabulary that this candidate lapses into on occasions.

12 Makes a useful comparison with Magwitch here in order to illustrate the point about Compeyson's immutably evil character.

13 A genuinely impressive analysis of imagery here. This shows good potential.

14 As with the introduction, the conclusion is signalled rather clumsily.

15 An effective summary of the points that have been explored regarding the main difference between these two characters.

16 Surprisingly sophisticated closing statement and, again, has effectively linked character and theme.

Compyson is the man who broke Miss Havisham's heart. He was born as a gentleman but never acts like one. Dickens is also using Compeyson to show that there is more to being a gentleman than being rich.**10** At the beginning of the book, not only has he stood**11** Miss Havisham up he has also betrayed Magwitch. Compeyson does not change during the novel as he also betrays Magwitch at the end of the novel by telling the police where they can find him. This is especially sad as Magwitch was just about to escape abroad with Pip. Because Pip is so fond of Magwitch, Dickens makes the reader like Magwitch too. So when Compeyson betrays him, the reader will hate him but then I don't think that we are meant to like him at any point in the novel. Magwitch was not a likeable character at the beginning but at least he becomes nice as the book goes on.**12** Compeyson is always evil which is why the reader is happy when Magwitch kills him. A good quote to show how evil Compeyson is is when Magwitch says in Chapter 42:

'He'd no more heart than a iron file, he was as cold as death, and he had the head of the Devil afore mentioned.'

Magwitch is comparing him to the Devil which shows how evil he is. I think that Magwitch also compares him to a file because that symbolises the connection between them as they are both prisoners at the beginning of the book.**13**

In conclusion,**14** Pip becomes a gentleman and then changes, becoming mean and unpleasant to Joe and Biddy who had looked after him when he was young. But then he changes again and is sorry for the way he treated them. Compeyson is not sorry at all and so he deserves to die.**15** Dickens shows with these characters that being a gentleman is not all what it is cracked up to be. As Biddy tells Pip in Chapter 19, 'a gentleman should not be unjust…' And this is what the novel is really all about!**16**

Grade-A* answer

In writing this bildungsroman,**1** Dickens is sending out a message to his society that the value of a person cannot be measured by the size of their bank account or by the rise in their social status.**2** Therefore, characters that grow to understand this are presented more sympathetically as they move closer towards this state of enlightenment. Such characters include Pip and Estella. Characters that stay the same are either presented sympathetically or with hostility depending on the degree to which they conform to Dickens' interpretation of moral perfection.**3** Pumblechook, for example, represents greed and hypocrisy and so Dickens' treatment of him remains hostile throughout the novel, even to the point of taking delight in the violent robbery of his premises by the villain Orlick. However, such static characters as Joe and Biddy are always presented with love and affection because of their outstanding good nature. They represent to the reader a vision of moral perfection because they are not affected by the shallow notions of class, or the lust for wealth, which is the novel's main social focus.**4**

Estella**5** makes tremendous growth during the course of the novel and, like Pip, her growth is based on painful experience caused by others. However, unlike Pip, her development into a full moral being is only revealed in the final pages.**6** This is because, although a main character, 'Great Expectations' is not really her story but Pip's. Whereas Pip's function as a character is to illustrate the corrupting power of class, her function is more to reveal the damage that misguided adults can do to children.**7** She is a victim before the novel has even begun and, therefore, wins much sympathy from the reader. However, the reader's first impression of her will not be favourable owing to Dickens' presentation of her as a spoilt and cruel child who takes delight in humiliating the good natured, but innocent and naive, Pip.**8** This will alienate her from the reader who has been encouraged to sympathise with Pip because of the many hardships that he has so far had to endure — and because of the admirable courage with which he does endure them. When Estella and Pip first meet, she is just another hardship.**9**

One of the ways that she demeans Pip is through belittling him because of his lower social status such as, in Chapter 8, when she calls him 'a common labouring-boy!' What particularly repels the reader is not so much the words themselves as their impact on Pip.**10** Dickens suggests the extent of this distress by the physicality with which he describes Pip's futile attempts to subdue his sense of shame: 'I got rid of my injured feelings for the time, by kicking them into the brewery wall, and twisting them out of my hair...'.**11**

1 Uses excellent technical term: bildungsroman.

2 Immediately relates the novel to its social, cultural and historical context.

3 Establishes awareness of authorial intent: that characters are creations of the author and are being used to achieve specific effects or to convey particular ideas.

4 An excellent introduction that provides an overview of Dickens' use of static and dynamic characters and has remained focused on the essay question. Clearly relates Dickens' use of characterisation to his intention to make an important social comment.

5 Now addresses the part of the question that focuses on two characters only.

6 Makes sophisticated comparisons between characters.

7 Excellent awareness of authorial intent: how Dickens uses Estella to develop a major theme.

8 Begins to address the part of the question that asks you to analyse the ways that Dickens presents characters that change.

9 Displays excellent awareness of how sympathy deliberately created for one character can create antipathy for another.

10 Excellent awareness of how Dickens is using characterisation to create an emotional impact on his reader.

11 Effective use of a short embedded quotation to illustrate the point being made.

12 Displays a clear awareness of a sophisticated interpretation of Estella that a lesser candidate might have missed.

13 Again, clear awareness that characters are constructs used by writers for specific purposes and are not real people.

14 Addresses the part of the question that requires the candidate to show an understanding of how this character has changed.

15 Again, an effective use of a short embedded quotation to prove the point being made.

16 Excellent awareness of the impact of the novel on both contemporary and modern readers.

17 Excellent analysis of Dickens' use of language to influence the reader.

18 Again, excellent use of technical terminology. A foil is a minor character who, by contrast, provides an insight into the personality of a main character.

19 Again, shows an excellent understanding of Dickens' authorial intent.

20 Yet another example of this candidate's ability to display a broad understanding of the novel while still focusing on only two characters.

However, the corrupting influence of the misguided adult in the background is clearly a mitigating feature.**12** Dickens shows the source of Estella's spiteful behaviour when he has Miss Havisham cruelly whisper 'You can break his heart'. Thus she makes a victim of two children at the same time.**13** Pip spends half of the novel deluded and seeking a worthless position in life so as to be worthy of the shallow notions of class superiority which Miss Havisham has forced upon Estella. And Estella drifts into a miserable marriage because she is incapable of feeling and so lacks direction.

By the end of the novel, she has finally developed the ability to both love and appreciate love**14** when she passionately remarks to Pip that she had rejected his love when she 'was quite ignorant of its worth'.**15** Dickens is satisfying his readers' (both past and present) longing for a positive resolution to what has so far been a one-way romance.**16** Estella's ultimate appreciation of Pip's value as a human being creates enormous compassion for her as it accords with the reader's own estimation of Pip by now. The use of the metaphor 'I have been bent and broken…into a better shape' further engages the reader's sympathy because it enables Dickens to represent the hardships that she has experienced in a most concrete and visual form. The words 'bent' and 'broken' are particularly emotive because they convey a sense of the violence she must have been exposed to in her marriage to the high born but brutal Drummle. The alliteration used helps to further increase the impact of these words on the reader while simultaneously conveying a most appropriate impression of romantic poeticism.**17**

One of the sympathetic characters that remains the same throughout the novel is Biddy and it is quite clear that Dickens is using her innate moral wisdom as a foil**18** to expose the moral shortcomings of Pip, Estella and, indeed, society at large.**19** As a result of her constancy she is a less complex character but her moral stature makes her crucial to the fundamental message that Dickens wants to convey to his readers. As Biddy tells Pip in Chapter 19, 'a gentleman should not be unjust…'. And when Pip is unjust towards her, accusing her of showing 'a bad side of human nature', the reader's disapproval once more helps Dickens to advance his theme that being a gentleman is more about good behaviour than wealth and rank — a lesson that Pip will spend much of the rest of the novel learning for himself.**20**

At the end of the novel, Biddy remains the same person as before — innately wise, compassionate and loving.**21** The only difference is that she has transferred her affections from Pip to Joe, a more equal match because he too has the same innate natural goodness and wisdom. Dickens uses their marriage as a further indication of Pip's own spiritual growth when Pip passionately remarks that Joe and Biddy are 'in charity and love with all mankind...' (Chapter 58), a striking contrast to the disparaging comments he had made about Biddy back in Chapter 19.**22** The explicit message that Dickens is sending out to his readers is that those who are willing to be guided by the principles of love and compassion, either through instinct or through having acquired them through experience, will have a much happier resolution than those whose only motivation in life is self-advancement.**23** In this way, 'Great Expectations' is a novel which transcends its own time and still speaks to the readers of today.**24,25**

21 Remains focused on the essay question, here displaying an awareness of the fact that, unlike Estella, Biddy does not change.

22 Excellent awareness again of how these more minor characters are being used by Dickens to reflect upon the spiritual progress of his main character.

23 Another example of this candidate's continual awareness of Dickens' social purpose in writing the novel.

24 Powerful concluding sentence in which the candidate shows an astute awareness of why the novel has remained relevant to modern readers.

25 Has written more about Estella than Biddy so the essay is not balanced. However, this is perfectly acceptable because, as the candidate has acknowledged within the essay, Estella is a much more complex character and therefore requires a greater degree of analysis.

Edexcel

Higher-tier theme-based question

> The approximate amount of time to spend on this question is 50 minutes. Read the extract from Chapter 19, p. 149, which begins 'Hear me out...' and ends '...if you have the heart to think so'.
>
> Answer all parts of the question that follows as fully as possible.
>
> a) Explain how the writer presents the character of Pip in this extract. Use evidence from the extract to support your answer. **(8)**
>
> b) Comment on the effect of the language used to show the relationship between Pip and Biddy in the extract. Use evidence from the extract to support your answer. **(10)**
>
> c) Explore the importance of social class in this extract. Use evidence from the extract to support your answer. **(10)**
>
> d) Explore the importance of social class in one other part of the novel. Use examples of the writer's language to support your answer. **(12)**
>
> **(Total: 40 marks)**

This question addresses both characterisation and theme. As we have already looked at a character-based question in the AQA student essays, the following responses address only part c) of the question. However, do remember that in the real Edexcel examination you are required to *answer all parts of the question*.

1 Begins with a good understanding of how Pip's rise in social status has made him a much less attractive character.

2 Shows a clear understanding of the fact that Dickens is using Pip to make a point to the reader.

3 Displays a rudimentary understanding that Dickens intentionally develops theme through a combination of characters and relationships in order to persuade the reader to his own moral point of view.

4 Simplistic vocabulary but does convey the point clearly enough.

Grade-C answer

c) Dickens is showing the reader that Pip has already become a snob because he knows that he is going to become a gentleman.**1** Dickens wrote the novel to say to the reader that being a gentleman does not mean that you have to look down on everybody as Pip is doing here to Biddy.**2** Pip is also rather rude about Joe, saying that he could do better. Biddy sticks up for Joe and I reckon that the reader probably would as well because Joe has always been good to Pip.**3** This change in Pip shows that being a gentleman can make you mean and look down on other people.**4**

Because Pip behaves badly, the reader can see that it is not always a good thing to become a gentleman.**5** Dickens is telling the reader that class can separate people and make them unpleasant to each other when they should be friends. Class is important in this passage because it breaks up people who used to be fond of each other and makes them strangers.**6** It also makes you look down on other people just because you are richer and Dickens does not like this.**7,8**

5 Starting to become repetitive now.

6 Addresses the question directly.

7 Shows a clear understanding of what Dickens is trying to say through his use of this theme.

8 Has used PEE (point, evidence, explanation) reasonably effectively in this response but if the candidate had also used quotation as evidence then it would have been possible to make higher scoring points about how Dickens uses language in order to develop theme. The lack of quotation means that the candidate has restricted this response purely to Dickens' use of character to develop theme.

Grade-A* answer

c) It is in Chapter 18 that Pip learns of his 'great expectations'.**1** In this extract from Chapter 19, Dickens is clearly illustrating that the corrupting power of class is instantaneous.**2** Prior to Pip's supposed good fortune, Biddy had been Pip's close friend, confidante and teacher and, consequently, he had had good reason to treat her with respect. However, as this extract clearly indicates, Pip's sudden elevation to a gentleman means that he already regards himself as Biddy's social superior and thus is losing sight of the ties which should bind them together, the most important one of which is their shared humanity.**3**

The extract opens with the peremptory statement 'Hear me out —', exactly as if Pip were addressing a subordinate.**4** This is followed by the condescending**5** reference to removing Joe 'into a higher sphere'. In one sense, Pip could be congratulated on his desire to repay Joe's constant affection and kindness towards him but, equally, Pip shows a singular lack of understanding of the man that he has lived with since he was a child.**6** Joe takes a pride in his work. And, furthermore, all that Pip is proposing to offer in the place of Joe's craftsmanship is an idle and insubstantial existence based on a stroke of good luck which has come from who knows where.**7** This fact not only indicates Pip's status bound snobbery but also his immaturity. A wiser person would realise that a gift of money from an unknown source is no foundation for a secure future.**8** Of course, Dickens ensures that this is a lesson that Pip will later have to learn.**9**

1 Briefly explains the context of the passage in order to establish its significance.

2 Quickly addresses the question.

3 Makes a powerful point about the impact of class, amply supported by reference to the text using an accurate paraphrase.

4 Excellent use of a short quotation, followed by subtle analysis of language.

5 This candidate's excellent vocabulary enables him/her to make precise judgements about character.

6 Excellent acknowledgement of alternative interpretations.

7 Displays an in-depth knowledge of how Dickens handles the theme of being a gentleman elsewhere in the novel.

8 A most imaginative and well-argued analysis of how Pip's personal development is being retarded by his new social status.

9 Displays a clear awareness of authorial intent.

10 Clear understanding of how Dickens uses character to develop theme.

11 Introduces a perceptive interpretation of Dickens' possible social message but qualifies it with an apt and imaginative reference to Dickens' own life; an impressive understanding of the historical context of the novel.

Biddy clearly expresses Dickens' view**10** regarding the value of life as a skilled artisan when Biddy comments that Joe 'may be too proud to let any one take him out of a place that he is competent to fill, and fills well and with respect'.

This is a most intriguing comment. It certainly promotes a life of industry over one of idleness but it could also be viewed as affirming that class distinctions are immutable and that people should not strive to break out of the class to which they were born. There seems to be a contradiction here between fiction and reality because, as is generally well known, Dickens was most dissatisfied with his own lowly position in life when, as a twelve-year-old, he was forced to work in a shoe blacking factory. On being rescued, he actively sought education in order to lift himself into a social sphere well beyond that of his own birth.**11**

Review your learning

(Answers on p. 93)

1 Your exam questions on *Great Expectations* will either be based on character or _____ ?
2 What can you use in order to shorten unnecessarily long quotations?
3 In which section of this guide can you learn more about essay planning and using PEE?
4 Dickens creates characters who undergo change and characters who remain _____ ?
5 Why does Dickens encourage the reader to dislike selfish characters?
6 In what way is *Great Expectations* still relevant to the modern reader?

More interactive questions and answers online.

Answers

Answers to the 'Review your learning' questions from each of the earlier sections.

Context (p. 12)

6 1812–70.
7 Pip's home town is based on Rochester.
8 1822.
9 Charles Dickens' father was imprisoned for debt and Charles Dickens had to work in a shoe blacking business.
10 Dickens had a love affair with Ellen Ternan.
11 He is stressing the importance of moral behaviour through Pip's progress in the novel.

Plot and structure (p. 27)

1 1807.
2 Seven.
3 Fourteen or fifteen.
4 'Suspense' means creating questions in the reader's mind which can only be answered by reading on.
5 To prevent the reader from becoming bored or frustrated.
6 They delay the main action and, therefore, the answers to the big areas of suspense.

Characterisation (p. 38)

1 A character's actions; a character's dialogue and what other people say about that character; a character's thoughts; the narrator's observations about a character; imagery.
2 'Charactonym' is the technique of giving characters names which reflect their personality and/or appearance.
3 All of them.
4 As a child he is naive and innocent. After he comes into his 'great expectations', he becomes elitist and egocentric. After he discovers who his real benefactor is, he starts to care about other people again.
5 Miss Havisham is a victim of Compeyson's cruel betrayal of her on her wedding day. Estella is a victim of Miss Havisham's desire for revenge.
6 Magwitch represents the essential nobility of the common man.

Themes (p. 47)

1 Gentility and social class, education, justice and mercy, romantic love, forgiveness and redemption.
2 Victorian society can be seen as unjust, class ridden and materialistic.
3 All of them!
4 Miss Havisham.
5 Social class, education and romantic love.
6 Miss Havisham, Mrs Joe and Arthur.

Style (p. 57)

1 A writer's style comprises the distinctive characteristics of their work that help to make that writer unique.
2 There are two narrative voices — the ironic voice of Dickens and the more romantic voice of Pip.
3 Places are often used symbolically.
4 Some of the techniques that Dickens uses in order to create humour include slapstick comedy, exaggeration, ludicrous behaviour and speech, irony, juxtaposition, incongruity, imagery and puns.
5 Mrs Joe is not treated seriously. This is because she is neither morally virtuous like Biddy nor tragically flawed like Miss Havisham and Estella.
6 Because Orlick's violence is meant to be frightening and not humorous.

Tackling the assessments (p. 73)

1 AQA and Edexcel.
2 AQA: examination in GCSE English Literature or Controlled Assessment Task in GCSE English Literature; Controlled Assessment Task in GCSE English Language. Edexcel: examination in GCSE English Literature only.
3 Read the question carefully and plan your answer.
4 Point, Evidence and Explanation.
5 Separate and embedded quotations.
6 You can refer to events in the text by paraphrasing.

Assessment Objectives and skills (p. 81)

1 The AQA GCSE English Literature Controlled Assessment Task.
2 According to how well you have addressed the relevant Assessment Objectives.
3 You have to demonstrate your understanding that authors create characters for particular purposes, such as to develop themes.

4 Simply retelling the story; quoting long passages; identifying techniques used by an author without explaining what the possible intended effect of these techniques is on the reader; giving unsubstantiated opinions — opinions not backed up by evidence.

5 To prove to the examiner that your opinion is valid.

6 The time period in which they live, their age, their nationality, their ethnic background and their life experience.

Sample essays (p. 90)

1 Theme.

2 Ellipsis.

3 Tackling the assessments.

4 The same/static.

5 Because he wants to promote a caring and compassionate society.

6 Because it deals with such eternal issues as morality, unrequited love and the struggle to discover a purpose in life.